ACTION AT THE BITTERROOT

When the bullet-blasted body was brought back to town, Brad Hollister recognized his friend, Tom King. King had struck a bonanza gold mine and had been on his way to file a claim when he'd been gunned down. Now only the killer knew where the mine was. Brad was sure he knew the murderer. To prove it, he took a deputy's badge and set out to find the mine—and trap the killer. There was just one hitch: the killer knew he was coming and lay in wait somewhere on the trail . . .

ACTION AT THE BITTERROOT

Paul Evan Lehman

CURLEY LARGE PRINT
HAMPTON, NEW HAMPSHIRE

Library of Congress Cataloging-in-Publication Data

Lehman, Paul Evan.
    Action at the Bitterroot / Paul Evan Lehman.
        p.   cm.
    ISBN 0–7927–1447–4 (Hardcover)
    ISBN 0–7927–1446–6 (Softcover)
    1. Large type books.   I. Title.
[PS3523.E434A64   1993]   92–37076
813′.54—dc20   CIP

British Library Cataloguing in Publication Data available

This Large Print edition is published by Chivers Press, England, and by Curley Large Print, an imprint of Chivers North America, 1993.

Published by arrangement with Donald MacCampbell Inc.

U.K. Hardcover ISBN 0 7451 1794 5
U.K. Softcover   ISBN 0 7451 1796 1
U.S. Hardcover ISBN 0 7927 1447 4
U.S. Softcover   ISBN 0 7927 1446 6

CHAPTER ONE

Bradford Hollister broke camp with the annoying knowledge that he was lost. He had left Briscoe with the thought that a short cut straight across the hills would get him to Juniper in about half the time required when following the winding stage road.

He realized now that the path he had been following was far from a straight line. He had left Briscoe on what should have been an easy day's ride, but a heavy blanket of low-hanging clouds had hidden the sun, and east might as easily have been west, north, or south. Darkness bogged him down on a rock flat, and now as he swallowed his third cup of breakfast coffee, the sky was brightening in the direction he had thought to be north.

Brad Hollister was a tall young man with the broad chest and slim waist of a greyhound. He had steady blue eyes, a tousled head of coppery brown hair, and a dimple which he tried to hide by not smiling unless he had to.

He cleaned up his breakfast utensils, saddled up, and headed directly south. The terrain was rugged and progress was slow, and it was close to noon when he heard the first shot. It came faintly from ahead, and his only reaction was the thought that at last he

1

was nearing some inhabited place. Two minutes later he heard another shot, still ahead but much more distinct. He was climbing the slope of a rocky ridge when the third shot came. A rifle shot.

He reached the crest of the ridge and pulled up. At the bottom of the slope and about a half-mile distant, a road snaked through scattered boulders, some of them as large as a two-story house. In the middle of the road lay a brown mass which was not a rock. It was a horse, a dead one.

Below and to his left Brad saw a man leap from one clump of rocks to another. He was a heavy man, but light on his feet, and he wore the slouch hat and flannel shirt of a miner. His features were partially hidden by his heavy black beard and a mustache. He was carrying a rifle.

The man got his footing and turned so that his back was toward Brad. The rifle whipped up, steadied, cracked, and Brad saw chips fly from a rock cluster a short distance from the dead horse. It was a safe bet that a man crouched behind those rocks, and since he did not answer the shot, it was a good guess that he was without a rifle.

Brad made another guess. A horseman had been riding along the road and Blackbeard had fired on him from ambush. The bullet had killed the horse, and the traveler had taken refuge amid the rocks. The horse had

2

probably fallen on the saddle boot, and the man had had no chance to get his rifle. Now Blackbeard had him pinned down in the rocks while he worked his way to a place from which he could shoot down at the hidden man. Blackbeard had not seen or heard Brad ride over the ridge.

Brad drew his rifle from the boot. For all he knew, the man in the rocks might need extermination, but until he was certain, his sympathies were with the hunted one. He saw that person leap out from the rocks and run toward the dead horse. Instantly Blackbeard whipped up his rifle and cut loose. The runner stopped, reeled slightly, then ran back to his shelter.

Brad started down the slope, and this time Blackbeard heard him and wheeled. Brad halted the horse, ready for a snap shot if the other made a hostile move. The fellow started to raise his rifle, then, realizing that he was out of accurate shooting range, turned and ran back, angling down the slope, throwing an occasional glance at Brad over his shoulder.

Brad saw a head pop up from behind the rocks, then the man left the shelter and ran to the dead horse. He bent over, tugged, came erect with a rifle in his hands. He fired and kept shooting until the magazine was empty. But Blackbeard, having reached his horse, kept in the protection of the rocks and quickly spurred from sight into a gully.

Brad pulled up beside the man who sat seated on a stone, dabbing at the top of his head with a handkerchief.

'Put a part in my hair,' he said to Brad, 'but it runs east and west instead of north and south. It isn't too bad. He was shooting downhill.'

Brad dropped off the horse and seated himself on another stone. 'Why was he trying to pot you?'

Grave brown eyes surveyed him, and Brad returned the gaze. He was looking at a strong, rugged man in his forties who had the lines of hard work carved on a whisker-stubbled face as dark as an old saddle. The heavy sweat-damp hair was sun-bleached. Flat-heeled hobnail boots, flannel shirt, and slouch hat which lay on the ground beside him said he was a miner.

'The only name I know him by is Jake,' the miner said. 'He was hiding on the slope and took a shot at me. I jerked my horse to a stop, and the bullet missed me and killed the cayuse. I had to get behind the rocks in a hurry. Pretty soon he would have been pumping lead right into my nest. He was out of pistol range and would have got me if you hadn't come along. I sure am obliged to you.' He thrust out a hand. 'The name is Tom King.'

Brad shook the man's hand. 'Bradford

4

Hollister. Tried a short cut across the hills from Briscoe and got lost. I'm headed for Juniper.'

'This road will take you there. I'm going to Sage City and have to pass through Juniper to get there.'

'I'll give you a lift as far as Juniper.'

They got the saddle and bridle off the dead horse, then dragged it to one side of the road. They hid the rig in the rocks; then Tom King got up behind Brad, and they set out for Juniper. Brad told the man what had brought him to this part of the country.

'Looking for some good range and a buy in cattle. I've held the job of marshal in several towns during the past few years and saved some money. Know of anything around here?'

'Well, there's plenty of free range, and cows are cheap since the panic. You shouldn't have any trouble stocking up. I started out as a cattleman myself. Homesteaded on a quarter-section on the Bitterroot some ten miles from Juniper right after the Homestead Law was passed in '62. When my wife died, I sent my daughter to an aunt in the East, sold my stock and most of the furniture, locked up the house, and went to prospecting. Too many memories in that house for me. I took out enough dust and nuggets to keep and educate Judy. She finished school last spring and expects to go to teaching.'

5

'She's your only child?'

'That's right. Here's her picture.'

The photograph showed a bright-eyed young woman in a lacy white dress standing beside a leather-faced man in store clothes whom Brad identified as Tom King.

'Taken when she graduated,' Tom explained. 'I went without eating to get the fare East for the occasion. Haven't seen her since.'

'She's right pretty,' said Brad, and passed the picture back.

They talked some more, and Brad found himself liking the man who rode behind him. Tom King was well-read and intelligent and seemed to return Brad's liking, but Brad noticed that he checked himself sharply when the conversation threatened to become personal. He acted as if he possessed a secret that he wanted to share but refrained from doing so because the man he rode with was a complete stranger.

When they came to a spring Brad split his saddle rations with Tom. Three hours later they came to a shallow basin, and Tom told Brad that Juniper lay just beyond the low range of hills on its farther side.

'We ought to get there right around dark, and I'll hire a horse and saddle from Duke Fisher and keep right on to Sage. Want to be there by morning. I'll finish my business and head right back to Juniper. If things turn out

6

the way I expect them to, I'll feel like celebrating. You stay around town until I get back and we'll tie on a good one.'

'I'll be there,' promised Brad.

At dusk they rode into Juniper. It was a thriving town with a general store, harness and boot shop, livery corral, barber shop, hotel, restaurant, a bank, and three saloons. One of the latter bore a sign proclaiming it the Happy Chance, *Duke Fisher, Prop*.

'Quite a place,' observed Brad, nodding toward it.

'Yes. Duke Fisher owns it. He also owns the store, the livery corral, and the hotel. Duke's a gambler; he'll take a chance on anything, and he's generally lucky. Made his pile on the stock market.'

'I thought the market went to pot in the panic.'

'I reckon Duke got out in time. Like I said, he's lucky. I've got to see him about a horse and saddle, but we'll eat first.'

They rode to the hitching rail in front of the Elite Cafe, dismounted, and went into the restaurant. A customer sat at the counter, forking beans into his mouth with a knife; two men were seated at one of the tables. The waiter-proprietor-cook was behind the counter, shooing flies away from a dried apple pie. Tom King's gaze was on the two men as he and Brad seated themselves at a table.

'That's Duke Fisher,' he told Brad in a low

7

voice. 'The one with the waxed mustache. The other is Phil Bronson; he owns the Cattlemen's Bank.'

Brad guessed that Duke Fisher was around thirty. He had dark hair and a pointed mustache and the white complexion of a man who spends most of his time indoors. He wore a black broadcloth coat and a dressy white shirt. On a chair was a broad-brimmed black hat. Phil Bronson, the banker, was a thin man with a pinched face, sharp eyes, thin lips, and a slightly hawkish nose. The two talked in low voices while they ate.

The waiter-proprietor-cook came around the counter to Brad's table. He made a swipe at a fly with a cloth and asked, 'What'll it be, gents?'

'The best you got,' said Tom, 'and plenty of it. Steak, hashed brown potatoes, stewed tomatoes—the works.' He gave Brad a slight grin. 'It's on me, Brad. Reckon I wouldn't be eating anything if it hadn't been for you.'

The restaurant man went into the kitchen. The bean-eater scooped up the last of his fare and went around the counter to cut himself a piece of pie. He refilled his coffee cup and returned to his place. Duke Fisher and the banker finished their supper and got up. They put money on the table, got their hats, and started for the door.

'Good evening, Tom,' said the banker as they passed.

8

'Howdy, Phil. Duke, I want to see you about hiring a horse.'

'Later,' said Duke Fisher shortly. 'I'll be at the hotel.'

He followed Bronson through the doorway and into the gathering darkness.

'Something's eating him,' Tom said.

The bean-eater finished his pie and coffee, put money beside his plate, and went out.

'Does Fisher live at the hotel?' asked Brad.

'Lives there and owns it. It's not fancy, but clean.'

They ate in silence, then Tom paid the owner and they went out into the darkness of early evening. Brad untied his horse and led it as they walked along the street toward the hotel.

'I'm mighty grateful to you, Brad,' said Tom gravely. 'You sure enough saved my bacon today. I'll try to make it up to you when I get back from Sage City.'

'Put off the trip until tomorrow and I'll ride along with you,' offered Brad.

'Can't do it. I've got to be there first thing in the morning. I just won't rest comfortable until—' Again he broke off, but he continued after a short pause: 'My business won't take long, and I'll start right back. Ought to get here shortly after noon. I can tell you then what took me there and maybe put you in line for something mighty good. Here's the hotel. There's a stable in back where you see the

9

lantern burning. Put up your horse and feed him, and I'll tell the clerk to have a room ready for you.'

They halted, stood for a moment gazing at each other in the semi-darkness. 'See you tomorrow afternoon,' said Tom King.

'I'll be around.'

Brad sensed rather than saw Tom's extended hand; he took it and they shook briefly.

'So long,' said Tom.

'So long,' echoed Brad.

It should have been good-by.

CHAPTER TWO

Duke Fisher and Phil Bronson sat in Duke's hotel room.

'It's just like I told you, Duke,' Phil said. 'I can't carry these mortgages any longer. You've made no payment on the principal; you haven't even kept up the interest. The panic hit me hard, too, and I've got to collect every cent I can to keep in business.'

'Don't give me that,' Duke said shortly. 'You invest only in gilt-edged securities and you tighten up at the first signs of a panic. You've got enough gold in your vault right now to pay the national debt.'

Bronson's lips tightened. 'What I have and

what I don't have doesn't enter in this. You borrowed heavily on your Juniper holdings in an effort to hang on in the stock market. I told you to get out and take your loss, but you wouldn't listen, and they finally sold you out. I lent you ten thousand dollars when you couldn't have got it anywhere else in the world. Instead of paying it back, you've continued to feed it into the stock market.'

'The market is bound to rise. All I need is a little more time, Phil.'

'The market will rise for the simple reason that it can't sink any lower. But it will be a very slow recovery, and you'll lose even more before you begin to gain. No, Duke, this thing must be settled now. If you had made any effort to repay me, I might have gone along with you a little longer; but you haven't, and I can't.'

'I wanted to pay it back in one lump sum,' said Duke impatiently. 'This fooling around a dollar at a time isn't my way of doing business. I don't play penny ante, Phil; I like to sit in a game where the sky's the limit.'

'That may be all right for a gambler, but you can't run a bank that way. If that mortgage isn't paid up tomorrow, I'll have to foreclose.'

'The full ten thousand?' Duke cried. 'Phil, you know I can't raise that amount!'

Bronson studied him. The average citizen of Juniper was unaware that Duke Fisher had

11

been hit at all by the panic. He was a gambler and could run a mighty convincing bluff, but Phil thought it was a bluff, and he was determined to call it. If Duke had the money, he'd have to pay; if he did not have it, he'd have to come across with every dime he could scrape up. But now Phil was convinced that Duke was not bluffing, that he really could not raise the amount of the mortgage.

'You're really determined to sell me out, aren't you?' said Duke bitterly. 'Well, there's not a damned thing I can do about it.'

Phil said, 'I'll make you one concession, Duke. I don't want to foreclose; I don't know who would buy the Happy Chance, and I certainly don't want to run it. You pay me half the principal and the interest to date, and I'll extend that note of yours another six months.'

Duke made a helpless gesture. 'I can raise ten thousand as easily as I can five.'

'Make a try at it. I'll give you three days.'

He took his hat off the floor and stood up. Duke rose with him.

'Phil, I can't believe you'd do this.'

'I don't like to, but I must protect myself. You have three days to dig up five thousand and interest. I'm sure you can do it if you really want to. Good night.'

He opened the door and strode down the corridor. He had no intention of foreclosing without giving Duke every chance, and felt

12

sure that for once the bluffer had been outbluffed. If Duke had the five thousand salted away, he'd come across. If he was really broke, Phil would modify his demands. Phil felt a little proud of the way he had carried it off.

Duke stood for some seconds scowling at the door, then seated himself at his desk. Folks in Juniper considered him a wealthy man. They knew him to be lucky at cards and assumed he was just as lucky at playing the stock market. His deal with Bronson had been a confidential one, since Bronson ran the bank alone, for the panic had forced him to discharge his only bookkeeper.

He realized now that he should have kept up the interest payments instead of throwing good money after bad, but gambler that he was, he spent little time in recrimination. He played his cards as they fell and accepted his losses as stoically as he did his gains. He was finding it a bit tough, though, to see all his holdings slip through his fingers. Somehow he must raise that five thousand dollars within the three-day time limit.

At a knock on the door, he said, 'Come in,' and turned as Tom King entered.

'What is it, Tom?' Duke asked, without cordiality.

'I've got to ride to Sage City right away. I want to hire a horse and saddle.' Then Tom told him about the ambush.

13

'Why did this man you called Jake want to kill you?'

Tom did not answer for a moment. Caution had kept him silent while he was with Brad Hollister, but he had known Duke for years and considered him a friend. He had even lent Duke money when Fisher first came to Juniper. Now, of course, Duke was a wealthy man and too busy gathering money on the stock market to go digging for it in the hills.

He said at last, 'This Jake is a professional claim jumper. He'll run a man off a good claim if he can, and in some cases men have disappeared. Nothing has ever been proved against him, but your guess is as good as mine as to what became of them. He killed them, Duke, just like he aimed to kill me.'

'You've struck it rich?'

'Mighty rich. I couldn't believe it until I'd taken out more than ten thousand dollars' worth. A thick vein that I hit at several places without any signs of its petering out. This fellow Jake must have snooped enough to make him want to get rid of me and stake it for himself.'

Duke was thinking swiftly. If Tom had struck it that rich, he might lend him the money he needed. 'Did you have that ten thousand on you when he ambushed you?'

'No. I hid it. Didn't take much pains, because I didn't know this Jake was spying on me. Just scooped out a hole, put the sacks of

14

gold in it, and rolled a stone over the hole. You see, I aimed to file on the claim first, then fetch the gold into the bank. If I brought it in first, word would get around that I'd struck it rich, and somebody like Jake might bump me off and file on it himself.'

Duke did not show the excitement which gripped him. If he borrowed the money to pay off the mortgage, he'd merely be wiping out one debt by incurring another. On the other hand, if he could find Tom's hidden gold while Tom was in Sage City, he could take it, and the theft would be blamed on the man named Jake.

Tom went on, his voice shaking with excitement. 'Duke, if this claim is only half as good as I think it is, me and Judy will be fixed for life.'

'You've written to her about it?'

Tom King tapped his breast. 'Got a letter for her right here. Aim to mail it in Sage. But I got to file first; I got to make sure before I tell her anything. Now let me have that horse, and I'll start for Sage.'

Duke got up. 'Sure, Tom. Come down to the corral and take your pick.'

They walked down together, and Tom selected a short-coupled bay and a saddle that suited him.

'The hoss has just been fed and watered,' the hostler told him. 'Don't push him too hard for the first few miles.'

15

'I won't push him at all. I'm anxious to get to Sage, but not before folks are out of bed. I got all night, and I'll take it easy all the way.'

'Well, good luck,' said Duke. 'You'll need another horse, and if you like this one I'll give you a bargain. I'll see you.'

Outside the stable, Duke quickened his steps. He had to know where Tom had located his claim, but a direct question was unthinkable. And he'd need a detailed description in order to find the mine. Tom would have that description on his person for filing purposes.

In the hotel lobby, he spoke to the clerk: 'Harry, I'm not feeling so good. I'm going to take a hot whiskey sling and turn in. Get word to the Happy Chance that I won't be in tonight. I don't want to be disturbed, no matter who asks for me. Got it?'

He went to his room and hurriedly changed into levis, laced boots, and an old slouch hat. A lariat hung on a wall by the window, a means of escape in case of fire; he took it down and hooked it over his arm. He tucked a black scarf into a pocket and buckled on a Colt .45.

He locked the door behind him and tiptoed to a window at the rear of the hallway, squeezing through it to the roof of the lean-to behind the hotel. From there he dropped to the alley.

Leaving the lantern hanging near the stable

entrance, he rigged his horse in the dark. There was another horse in the stable, and he knew that the hotel had another roomer for the night. He led his own mount through a rear entrance, got aboard, and started across country toward a bend in the road beyond Juniper. Here he halted to listen. He heard the beat of hoofs from the direction of town, and turned his horse toward Sage City and put it to a canter. He rode steadily for two hours, then halted at the foot of a slope a short distance from the Bitterroot River. The road was lined on both sides with scrub pines and pin oaks. He dismounted and led his horse a short distance from the road and tied him, then returned, carrying the rope. He tied the honda end of the lariat to a tree on the far side of the road, recrossed, uncoiling the rope as he walked, and squatted on his heels beside another tree.

He took the slack out of the rope, drawing it taut at the proper height to trip Tom's horse. When the horse fell, Tom would be thrown over its head. When he landed, he might be momentarily stunned; if not, a tap on the head with a gun barrel should do the job. Then Duke would take the location papers and the letter to Judith King, start Tom's horse on the trail for home, and get back to Juniper before daylight. He'd sneak into his room, change clothes, have an early breakfast, then ride to the mine and get

17

Tom's gold. Nothing to it.

Eventually Tom would work his way back to Juniper. He'd be convinced that he had been waylaid by Jake, that the one who stole the papers was the same man who had ambushed him that morning.

In the distance, Duke heard the faint thud of hoofs.

He fastened the black scarf in place, thus concealing his lack of black beard and mustache.

Soon the vague forms of horse and rider rose against the sky at the crest of the ridge, then descended the trail. Duke shifted his position, made an experimental jerk, then let the rope go slack again. His gaze went to the swiftly moving bulk. Watch carefully, Duke! At just the right moment—!

Now! And he snapped the rope taut.

The horse slid on its knees, squealing; it fell on its side, rolled, then scrambled to its feet. Duke was not watching the horse; his gaze was on the rider who had been catapulted over its head. Tom landed on his chest, slid through the dust, then lay still.

Duke drew his gun and ran up. He rolled Tom on his back, put the gun on the ground, and thrust his hand into the inside coat pocket. His fingers touched the papers there. But then a fist came up, striking Duke in the face. He withdrew the hand and fastened it about Tom's throat. Instinctively Tom fought

18

back; and again a fist thudded into Duke's face. Duke toppled backward, letting go his hold. Tom was getting to his feet, and Duke knew that he would come up with a gun in his hand.

His hand closed on the gun he had laid down. He pushed himself to a sitting position just as Tom gained his feet and turned. Duke snapped up the Colt and fired, thumbing the hammer again and again. He was thumbing it on empty shells even after Tom fell.

CHAPTER THREE

Tom King lay on his back, legs spread, arms outflung. Duke knelt beside him, took a wrist in his left hand, felt no pulse; he put his cheek close to Tom's mouth and could detect no breathing. Duke was a good shot, and his bullets had traveled less than fifteen feet. Tom King was dead.

Duke holstered his gun and once more thrust a hand into the inside pocket. He drew out the papers, struck a match, and glanced at them. He was holding the letter addressed to Judith King and a sheet of paper upon which Tom had written the exact location of his claim. This was what Duke wanted. He dropped the match into the dust of the road and put both letter and location notice into his pocket.

An overwhelming urge to get out of there then seized him, and he got up quickly. He forced himself into some semblance of calm, reminding himself that he must leave nothing that would connect him with the shooting, but there was no time, for he must be back in Juniper before daybreak. Safer to leave things just as they were. The man Tom had mentioned—Bradford Something-or-other—would report the attack on Tom by the bearded miner, and Sheriff Rutherford would conclude that the claim jumper had again waylaid Tom and this time had murdered him.

Duke walked to the tree to which the rope was tied and worked at the knot. The impact of the running horse against it had tightened the knot, and his shaking fingers could not loosen it. He cut the rope close to the knot and ran to his horse, coiling the rope as he did so. He looped the lariat over the saddle horn, untied the horse, and mounted. He followed a course parallel with the road to the top of the ridge, then cut into the road and put his horse to a canter. The rush of wind as he rode cooled his nerves.

And now the full significance of Tom King's death reached him. Not only would the gold Tom had already taken from the mine be his, but also the whole mine! All he had to do was to outfit himself, go into the hills, and pretend that he had made the strike. Then he'd file on the claim, prove up on it, and be rich! Tom had not been over optimistic; if he said he had made a rich strike, that is what it was.

Duke left the stage road where he had entered it and made his way to the stable just as the sky was beginning to brighten in the east. He put the horse into its stall, climbed up, and crawled through the open window. In his room he hung the coiled rope on its wall nail and changed his clothes. He was tired but too highly strung to sleep. He lighted a lamp, sat down at his desk, and looked at the letter to Judith and the location notice, both perforated by his bullet. A quick study of the paper showed him that the mine was about a day's ride from Juniper and easily located.

The letter to Judith King was filled with the jubilation of a father who sees his dreams for his daughter realized. He had made a big strike, a strike that would make them both rich ... Duke put aside the letter and went back to the location notice. He sat at his desk a long time mulling over his plans.

Dawn came, and he heard movement downstairs. He blew out the lamp, got up, stopped in the act of returning letter and paper to his pocket. He must copy the location notice and then destroy both it and the letter. They were the only thing to connect him with Tom King's death.

21

He felt in his pockets for a match and found he had used the last one to light the lamp. There was a match safe on his desk, but it was empty. He shrugged. There was no hurry; he would copy it at the mine and burn the papers there. He put them into his pocket and went downstairs.

The clerk was making a fire in the kitchen stove. He grinned at Duke. 'Feeling better?'

'I feel fine,' answered Duke truthfully. 'Anybody ask for me?'

'Ed Carney came looking for you from the Happy Chance. I told him you'd turned in and wasn't to be disturbed and that he should close up the joint. That was all.'

Duke went to the stable, watered his horse, and rubbed him down. When he returned, Harry had his breakfast ready.

'I noticed another horse in the stable,' he said.

'Yeah. Belongs to a feller named Bradford Hollister. He got a room for the night.'

Duke nodded. 'That must be the man who fetched Tom King to Juniper after Tom got bushwhacked.'

'Huh?'

Duke told him about it. The more people who knew of that first attempt to kill Tom, the better. Then he said, 'I've got to ride out into the country on business. Probably won't be back tonight. Pack some grub for me. And when you get time, tell Ed to take over at the

22

Happy Chance.'

He ate a good breakfast, got a package of food from Harry, and put it into his saddlebags. He made up a bedroll, and strapped it behind the cantle, filled his canteen, and set out. He rode past Tom King's dead horse somewhere around noon and late that afternoon reached the claim. Everything was in his favor; the hiding place of the gold was as easy to find as had been the claim. Duke breathed easier when he uncovered the canvas sacks with their yellow contents; he had been a bit worried that the man Jake had found the treasure.

The claim lay in a dry creek bed, and Tom King had driven several drifts into the north bank. Duke went into one of these, lighting his way with a lantern hanging at the entrance. He came to a lateral tunnel and followed it, inspecting the rock wall until he found a niche containing loose stones and gravel and scooped them out. Hidden behind them was a wide vein of gold. At the end of the lateral he found another place where Tom had concealed the vein with rubble. He went back the way he had come and entered another drift farther along the creek. There were four drifts, each leading to a lateral tunnel, and in each of them he found a vein. He was sweating with excitement when he finally finished his examination. The vein showed no sign of pinching out, and under the law he could file on three thousand feet in any direction from the point of discovery.

The sun had gone, and Duke sat down on a stone, took off his hat, and mopped his forehead. There was no doubting it; here was a fortune for the taking...

★   ★   ★

Brad Hollister, after leaving Tom King, led his horse to the hotel stable and put him into a stall. There was one other horse in the stable, a handsome black, and Brad noticed him casually as he fed his own mount. He shouldered his bedroll, then went into the lobby of the hotel and introduced himself to the man behind the desk.

'Tom King told me you were putting up your horse,' said Harry. 'A room will cost you fifty cents, and there'll be two bits for the horse. We don't serve meals; you'll have to eat breakfast at the restaurant.'

Brad registered, took a key from the clerk, and went up to his room. He dumped his bedroll in a corner, washed up, and went out again. For lack of something better to do, he started to make a circuit of the town. When he came to the Happy Chance, he went inside. There was a fifty-foot bar with an expensive-looking mirror behind it, and a row of gaming tables. A few men stood at the bar, and five players sat around a poker table. The other games were idle; men simply did not have the money to gamble. The place was well furnished, a bit on the garish side, and it was lighted by three brass chandeliers, each holding a dozen small kerosene lamps.

As Brad stood just inside the doorway looking the place over, a big, rugged man at the bar turned casually and looked at him, then started toward him, his hand extended.

'Bless my soul, if it ain't Brad Hollister!'

Brad shook the hand. 'That's right. And you're Sheriff Rutherford. I remember you were from somewhere around here. Sage City, wasn't it?'

'Sage is the county seat, but Juniper's in my jurisdiction. Had to let my deputies go when the panic hit, so I'm in the saddle most of the time. Might as well be punching cows. How are you, Brad?'

'Fine as frog's hair.'

'Looking for somebody around here? If you are, you can count on my help. I never would have caught up with that killer if it hadn't been for you.'

'I'm not a lawman any more, John. I turned in my badge, and right now I'm looking for some range and a good cattle buy.'

'Plenty of good grass around here, and you ought to be able to pick up cows right cheap. Come over and have a drink.'

They went to the bar and ordered. They

drank to each other's health, and Brad ordered another round.

'Going to be in Juniper for a spell?' Rutherford asked.

'A few days, anyhow. Do you know a miner named Tom King?'

'Sure. He has a homestead on the Bitterroot, but took to prospecting after his wife died. Got a daughter back East.'

'Know her?'

'Used to, years back. I know where she lives; Tom gave me her address in case anything happens to him. Where did you run into Tom?'

Brad told him about the ambush by the miner named Jake.

'That Jake is a claim jumper, all right,' said Rutherford. 'I've had complaints about him but never have been able to catch up with him. Did Tom say anything about striking it rich?'

'No, but he seemed plenty excited about something. And he was in a big hurry to get to Sage City. Rented a horse and saddle from Duke Fisher and started out right after supper. Wouldn't wait until morning.'

'H'm. That and Jake's trying to kill him tell me powerful loud that he made a rich strike. I'll bet a stack of blues he was anxious to get to Sage to file on his claim. Well, I wish him luck; Tom's a good, hard-working man and all wrapped up in that girl of his.'

26

He tossed off his drink, wiped his mustache. 'Reckon I'll be turning in, Brad. Want to get an early start for Sage, myself. And while I'm gone you're welcome to use my cot and stable at the office. Save you a hotel bill. If you haven't anything better to do, ride over and pay me a visit. I live alone, and there's plenty room. Meanwhile, I'll keep my eyes and ears open for a good cattle buy for you.'

They went out together and walked to the little jail building, where the sheriff would spend the night, then Brad went on to the hotel stable. He watered his horse and got some hay from the loft, noticing that the black was no longer in its stall. Then he went up to his room, undressed, and turned in.

Brad, awake early, tried to go back to sleep but couldn't, so he got up and went downstairs. He headed for the back door, passing through the kitchen where the clerk was eating his breakfast.

'I'm going to feed my horse; want me to feed the other one while I'm at it?'

'Other one's gone. Belongs to Duke Fisher. He got business in the country and rode away ten minutes ago. Thanks just the same.'

Brad gave his horse a measure of oats, then went to the restaurant for his breakfast. While he was eating, he had the proprietor make up some sandwiches. He went back to the hotel, got his bedroll, paid for his

27

lodging, and saddled up. He rode to the jail but found that Sheriff Rutherford had left for Sage City. He'd take advantage of the offer and make this his home while in Juniper. Meanwhile, there was time to kill until the afternoon, when Tom King would return.

He rode westward at a leisurely gait. He saw a range he liked, and Rutherford had assured him he could find stock for it. He carried a little over a thousand dollars in his money belt, and he was ready to talk business if he came across a good buy.

After a few miles he came to a river which he guessed was the Bitterroot. He rode southward along its bank, passed the buildings of a ranch to his right, then saw a house and several small buildings on the bank of the river ahead of him. The country on this side of the Bitterroot was gently rolling, but on the other side the hills came clear to the river's edge. As he approached the ranch ahead of him, he had the impression that it was deserted. Tom King's abandoned homestead must be somewhere near here, he thought.

When he reached it, he was sure it was King's. The windows were boarded over, the doors padlocked. Tom had said the place held too many memories, and Brad was pretty sure he would not return here to live. He looked about and decided that this was the place he was looking for. Perhaps Tom would sell the homestead to him. He dismounted, tied his horse to a hitching post, and walked slowly around the main building.

It was built of logs and adobe, soundly constructed and roomy. Looking between the cracks of the boarded-up windows, he saw the kitchen was furnished and so was one of the bedrooms. He remembered Tom telling him that he had sold most of the furniture; he probably kept these two rooms for an occasional overnight visit.

On one side a pipe entered the house from the direction of the river. He followed it to the bank, where it disappeared under the surface of the water. Directly across the stream a spring gushed out of the face of a cliff some fifty feet above ground level, spilling into a pool at the base and then overflowing into the river. The pipe ran up the perpendicular rock wall, and Brad knew that the water flowed by gravity into the house. So Tom had running water, a luxury rarely enjoyed in cattle country. A branch pipe ran to a watering trough in the yard, but he found the flow had been cut off by a valve. Better and better.

He sat down on the little porch and ate his sandwiches. This was just the kind of place he wanted. He would talk to Tom about it when he met him this afternoon.

He mounted his horse and rode toward Juniper, dreaming a little. With the house and buildings would go a hundred and sixty acres which would be his land; if he needed more, the range was probably available for rent from the adjoining ranchers. He entered town around three in the afternoon, stabled his horse in the jail stable, and walked to the Happy Chance. He did not find Tom King waiting for him there and the bartender had not seen him. He drank a glass of warm beer and went outside.

Sheriff Rutherford rode into sight at the far end of the street. He was leading a second horse with something like a body draped over its back. As he came nearer, Brad could see the dangling, booted legs, but the upper part of the man's body was on the far side of the horse.

Men came out of houses and saloons and followed the sheriff along the street, calling questions. Brad heard Rutherford's terse answer.

'Found Tom King on the Sage road just this side of the Bitterroot Crossing. Somebody murdered him.'

CHAPTER FOUR

Brad walked out into the street and the sheriff halted.

'Who did it?'

'Your guess is as good as mine. Mine says it was Jake. He probably knew or guessed that Tom was heading for Sage and rode around Juniper to wait for him. He made a good job of it; five bullets through the body. Come along to the undertaker's with me; I want to talk with you.'

He clucked to his horse, and Brad fell in beside him. Rutherford pulled over to a picket fence beyond which was a scrawny lawn and a once-white cottage. On the lawn a board sign read: *W. B. Kline, M.D.*

'Doc is Juniper's undertaker as well as its medico. The boys say he kills his clients for a fee and then collects another one for burying them. You'll have to give me a hand.'

Together they got the dead man from his horse and carried him up to the cottage door. Dr. Kline had come out to the porch; he looked at the dead man, shook his head.

'Tom King, eh? Take him into the back room. Who did it, John?'

'I don't know. Found him on the Sage road.'

They laid Tom on the examination table and stripped off his clothing, Rutherford going through the pockets as they did so. He found a wallet containing forty dollars in bills and change amounting to two dollars and sixty cents. Around his waist was a money belt containing a thousand dollars in gold pieces. Rutherford gave the forty dollars to

31

the doctor.

'Fix him up and give him a good burial, Doc. I've got to go to Sage. Want to ride along, Brad?'

Brad saw the appeal in his eyes and said yes. Rutherford rode with him as he went to the jail stable to get his horse.

'I'm wondering,' said Brad, 'how Jake happened to overlook both the wallet and the money belt.'

'Must have been looking for bigger game. You'll notice there were no papers of any kind on Tom; yet if he was going to Sage to file on a claim, he must have had some notes about its location on him. That's what Jake wanted, those location notes. Why? Because, if they were found on Tom's body, and then later Jake located on the same claim, there'd be a plain case of murder against him.'

This was true enough, and Brad let it lie at that; but if Jake was a professional thief, it was not at all logical that he'd pass up the forty-two dollars in the wallet and the thousand in the belt. 'If there was a rich claim, Jake's next move would be to file on it himself,' he said.

'Maybe, maybe not. From what I hear, Jake never files on a claim; just works it out and leaves it.'

'If it was so rich that he'd murder a man to get it, he'd have to file to protect himself,' Brad pointed out. 'I figure it would be a good idea to keep an eye on the land office, and if a big blackbearded man tries to file, nab him and put him through the wringer. I've got a pretty good picture of him in my mind.'

'Good! That's why I want you to ride to Sage with me. Chances are he'll lay low for a while before filing, but if he does show up, we'll nail him.'

They set out for Sage City, and Rutherford halted Brad when they reached the place where he'd found Tom King.

'He was lying right there,' Rutherford said, pointing. 'You can see the dry patch of blood. I saw his saddled horse grazing beyond the ridge back there. Later, I found where the killer had tied his horse, back in the brush, and I found where the rope had been tied that tripped Tom's horse. Footprints around the body and in the road. The prints are too fuzzy, but they were the usual miner's boots.'

Brad swung off his horse. 'Let's take another look.'

He went to the tree the sheriff had pointed out and squatted down.

'Knot was so tight that he cut it instead of untying it,' said Rutherford. 'He was in a hurry.'

'It was a lass rope,' said Brad, 'tied at the honda end.'

'That means,' said Rutherford, 'that if we find a rope on Jake's saddle with the honda cut off, we'll have his hide nailed to the

33

fence.'

'Jake is a miner; miners don't usually carry ropes with hondas.'

'Maybe Jake's been doing a little cattle rustling on the side.'

It was late when they rode into Sage City, and the land office was closed, but they found the agent at his home. Nobody had filed a mining claim for several days. Brad described Jake as well as he could, and the man said he'd look for a miner answering the description.

'Just let him file,' Brad said, 'then pass the location on to me. We'll do the rest.'

They ate a late supper, then made a circuit of the town in a futile effort to find Jake. It was midnight when they went into John Rutherford's cottage.

'In the morning,' the sheriff said, 'I've got to do a job that I sure hate. I've got to write Judith King and tell her about her father and send her his thousand dollars. I'd better telegraph the money; she may need it.'

'Why not send her a telegram along with the money saying that her father passed away and that you're writing her the details. That will let her get kind of used to the idea before telling her he was murdered.'

'Good stuff, Brad. I'll do it, first thing in the morning.' He was silent then a moment, thinking, his steady gaze on Brad. Then he said: 'Are you doing anything special for the next week or two?'

'Not a thing. I saw Tom's homestead on the Bitterroot, and I'd like to have it. Maybe now Miss King will sell it to me. I'll wait until the shock has passed and write her. You want me to help you find Jake?'

'Brad, I'd be mighty grateful if you would. I can hire a man from day to day if I need one. You have the savvy and the experience, and I sure enough need some help. How about it?'

'I knew Tom King only a few hours, but I cottoned to him right away. I'll be glad to help run down his killer.'

Rutherford swore him in as a special deputy then and there. 'I don't have to tell you what to do, Brad. Use your own judgment.'

'Then I'll start hunting Jake. You'll probably be around Sage where you can keep in touch with the land office. I'll work out of Juniper, and if you have anything to tell me, come there or leave a message for me at the Happy Chance. If Tom was on his way to file a claim and Jake aims to file on it himself, he'll probably wait until he thinks it's safe before coming to Sage. He'll stick pretty close to Tom's claim while he's waiting. I'll ride back to the section where Tom was prospecting and snoop around.'

'You don't know where Tom located his claim. I don't, and nobody else except Jake does either, that I know of.'

'I'll start from where I first met Tom and backtrack. Tom carried no bedroll or saddle rations. I figure he was on the trail for only five or six hours when Jake shot his horse.'

They turned in then, and when they got up the next morning, Rutherford cooked breakfast for them. When they had eaten and cleaned up the dishes, Brad set out at once for Juniper.

*   *   *

Duke Fisher spent the night at the claim and started back to Juniper the next morning. Tom had put the dust and nuggets in canvas bags, and Duke put these into two gunnysacks, which he tied together by the necks, and draped them over his horse behind the saddle.

Tom's location notice and the letter to Judith remained in Duke's pocket. In his excitement following seeing the gold vein, he had at first forgotten them, and later he could find no paper on which to copy the location notice, so once more he postponed action. Besides, his chief concern now was to pay off the mortgages and get Phil Bronson off his neck.

He arrived in Juniper in the afternoon and halted his horse in front of the Cattlemen's Bank. He carried the gunnysacks into the bank and dropped them on the counter. Bronson was alone.

'The money is in these sacks, Phil,' Duke announced. 'Pretty nearly the whole amount. It's in dust and nuggets and just about pure gold. Weigh it up, and let's see what it's worth.'

Bronson opened a canvas sack and looked inside. He whistled softly. 'That's top-grade stuff, Duke. Where'd you get it?'

'I had a nice piece of luck. A year or so ago I grubstaked a miner. Every once in a while I take a long shot like that, as you probably know. This time it paid off.

'You gave me three days to raise five thousand dollars, and my only hope was this miner I'd grubstaked. I knew just about where he was working, and yesterday I rode out to see him. I found him getting ready to ride in to see me. He was all excited. He had found some rich pockets and had taken out twenty thousand dollars' worth. Half of that was mine.'

Phil Bronson started weighing out the gold. 'Going to fetch in some more like this?'

'I hope so; but I won't get it from Joe Hartwell.'

Bronson looked up. 'Joe Hartwell? I don't seem to remember him.'

'You wouldn't. Joe didn't come to town often. Got his supplies at Briscoe. And when he did come in he didn't circulate around.

37

Saw me and got out.'

'You said if you brought more in, you wouldn't get it from him. Why?'

'He quit the claim. Packed his ten thousand on a jackass and headed for Briscoe. He'd kept digging nearly a week after he found this and didn't find any more. He figured the claim had petered out. But I got the idea there's more where this came from, and I'm going up there and work it myself.'

Once more Bronson looked up at him. 'You? Prospect?'

'Why not? Business at the Happy Chance is off, and a little outdoor work won't hurt me.'

Bronson finished his weighing, did some figuring. 'Ten thousand two hundred and seventy dollars.'

'How close will that come to cleaning up the whole debt?'

'The principal is ten thousand; the interest amounts to something like eight hundred dollars. You haven't paid a cent, you know.'

'Keep it all. I can scrape together enough to pay the balance of the interest in a few days. Tell you what; why can't you cancel that mortgage note and let me give you another one for the rest of the interest? I tell you there's more gold there, and you're going to find me a pretty big depositor.'

Phil considered and agreed. Duke went out of the bank feeling pretty good. He left behind him a thankful and wondering banker.

Duke got on his horse and headed toward the hotel. Approaching him at a smart trot was a team of matched bays, and over their heads he could see Doc Kline on the driver's seat of the wagon he used as a hearse. Farther up the street men and women were coming from the direction of the town cemetery. He reined over to the nearest hitching post and slid to the ground. He could guess whose funeral it was, but he wanted to know the details.

A man strode alone in advance of the group of mourners. Unlike the rest, he was not wearing Sunday clothes; his attire was that of a cowman, carefully brushed but showing signs of daily wear. When he came nearer, Duke recognized him as the man who had been with Tom King in the restaurant. Duke stepped to the sidewalk and stopped him.

'Pardon me, sir; you're Bradford Hollister, aren't you?'

'That's right. And you're Duke Fisher.'

'Tom King told you, I suppose. He spoke highly of you; said you saved his bacon the other day. I've been out of town on business. Has Tom got back from Sage City yet?'

'He never reached Sage. Sheriff Rutherford found his body on the road halfway there. He'd been murdered; shot five times. He was just buried.'

'No!' Duke appeared to be shocked.

'Murdered! Who did it?'

'The best guess is that it was the same man who tried to kill him earlier that day. The claim jumper named Jake.'

Duke nodded. 'Of course. Tom told me about that. Poor Tom! He was a good man and a friend of mine. What is Rutherford doing about it?'

'For one thing, he appointed me a deputy to help find Jake. I saw him, and I'll recognize him if I see him again. When I rode into town it was just in time to follow Tom to the cemetery. I'm going to buy supplies and start for the hills.'

'I hope you find him,' said Duke, the sincerity in his voice real. 'Don't take any chances; he's bad. Shoot him down on sight!'

Brad nodded, left and cut diagonally across to the store.

Duke led his horse to the hotel stable. Rutherford was thinking just what Duke had expected him to think, and both he and Hollister would concentrate their efforts on finding the man named Jake. If they caught him, Jake would deny having killed Tom, but considering what had happened earlier in the day, he was doomed.

Duke went to the Happy Chance and gave his assistant, Ed Carney, instructions. 'Remember that miner, Joe Hartwell, who used to come in once in a while? I grubstaked him and he struck a pretty good prospect.

40

Took out twenty thousand and then quit cold. He thought he was rich and started for his home back East. I have a hunch there's more on that claim, and I'm going to work it.'

Ed lifted his heavy eyebrows. 'You, boss?'

'Any law against it? I can get just as lucky as Joe Hartwell. I'll be in from time to time to check with you. You'll draw an extra five bucks a week from now on. That suit you?'

'Sure, Duke! Don't you worry none; I'll take care of things.'

Duke went to his hotel room, locked the door, and seated himself at the desk. He got the location notice and the letter from his pocket and put them on the desk. He got paper and pen and copied the notice. Tomorrow he would go to the claim, check directions, landmarks and measurements and acquaint himself with the whole layout. Then he'd 'discover' the claim. But he'd let a week go by just in case Tom King had hinted to somebody that he'd struck it rich. If it were known that he had prospected around a week or so before finding the claim, and if later it was found that the claim had originally been discovered by Tom King, then Duke's discovery would be considered an accident, and that fact would not tie him in with Tom's murder.

Again he thought of destroying the papers, and again he found the match safe empty. Since he did not smoke, he carried no matches in his pocket. He put the papers back into his pocket. He must purchase supplies to take to the mine, not forgetting a carton of matches. After all, there was no hurry in burning the papers, as long as Rutherford and Hollister were intent on hunting Jake.

He gave the storekeeper a list of supplies and told him to pack the stuff in gunnysacks and have them ready for him in the morning. He related the same story he had told Phil Bronson and Ed Carney. The more people who knew of his prospecting, the better for his purpose.

'Another feller was just in to stock up,' said the storekeeper. 'Man named Hollister. You reckon he's going prospecting, too?'

'He's going prospecting, all right, but not for gold. Rutherford swore him in as a special deputy to find the man that killed poor Tom.'

He went to the restaurant and had his supper, then walked to the livery corral and told his man there to have a mule fed and ready the next morning.

'Put a pack saddle on her and take her up to the store and load the stuff I bought. Leave her there, and I'll pick her up on my way out.'

He went to the Happy Chance for a final check, spent some time chatting with customers, giving out the information that he was about to turn prospector but not saying

42

where he was going to prospect. He went to the hotel around ten; he wanted to get an early start the next morning. He repeated his story to Harry and told him to have breakfast ready at six.

He had bought matches, but they were with his supplies, and he had forgotten to ask Harry for some. Well, the hell with it. He felt in his pocket; the papers were still safe, and they would remain safe until he reached the mine. He undressed in the dark and went to bed.

CHAPTER FIVE

It was late in the afternoon after he left Duke Fisher, but Brad Hollister was anxious to get on Jake's trail. He went to the store and ordered supplies, then to the restaurant for an early supper. It was still light when he rode out of Juniper.

He rode along the Briscoe road, by which he and Tom had come to Juniper, and camped at the boulder-strewn place where Tom had been ambushed the first time. At his campfire he considered carefully before he turned in. Packing neither bedroll nor rations, evidently Tom had not expected to camp on his way to Sage City. It had been around noon, Brad remembered, when he had heard the first shot that day. If Tom had left his claim immediately after breakfast, he could not have been on the trail for more than six or seven hours before Jake jumped him.

The distance Tom had covered in those six or seven hours would depend a lot on the terrain he had traveled. The claim would be in the hills, and part of his ride would be through rugged country. If he averaged three miles an hour, the claim would be eighteen or twenty miles away from this place. But in which direction? Tom had been moving westward, so the claim would be either north, south, or east from here. The country Brad must cover would be in a rough half-circle some twenty miles in radius. That would be about fifteen hundred miles. Brad shook his head; a lot of territory for one man to search, but it had to be done.

Early the next morning he began his search. Assuming that Tom had entered the road from the hills, he set off toward Briscoe, scanning both sides of the road and exploring each entering trail he came to. One led to a burned cabin, another to a rockfall which barred further progress. Others led him to claims worked by miners who denied any knowledge of Tom's claim. Each time Brad returned to the road and continued the search.

He went on like this for a week; when his supplies were exhausted, he would have to return to Juniper for more. He had progressed less than a dozen miles from his starting point.

Emerging from a branch path to the road, he decided to press on just a little farther before heading for Juniper. An hour's ride brought him to a well-traveled path, and he turned into it.

Five miles from the road he found the first diggings. Unlike the other deserted claims, these appeared to have been worked within the last few months. Shafts had been sunk to bedrock before being abandoned, and the work had been careful and methodical. Excitement stirred Brad; he had a hunch that at last he was in Tom King's territory.

He was lucky enough to shoot a turkey for food, and he decided to keep going one more day. There were paths leading from these claims to others. Brad moved along them cautiously, aware that at any moment he might come across Tom's claim. And there, he was sure, he would find the big, blackbearded miner named Jake.

He rode into a dry creek bed and pulled to an abrupt halt. There were hoofprints in the gravel, and fresh horse droppings. The opposite bank rose steeply, and into it a horizontal drift had been dug. The dirt which had been removed from the tunnel lay in two piles before the entrance, and from that opening a man suddenly stepped.

45

They stared at each other a few seconds before recognition came to Brad. Duke Fisher did not look like the owner of the Happy Chance; he wore a prospector's soiled blue jeans and red flannel shirt, scuffed laced boots, and battered felt hat. A gun belt was buckled about him, and he held a big Colt pointed at Brad.

'It's you,' he said, shoving the gun back into its holster.

'That's right,' answered Brad, and rode down into the creek bed. He swung off, looked up and down the dry wash, then at Duke. 'Is this your claim?'

'It is.'

'I didn't know you were a prospector, but it looks as though you've been working on it for quite a while.'

'Just this week. Before that it was worked by a miner I grubstaked, Joe Hartwell. He took out twenty thousand and called it quits. I took up where he left off. Had a little luck, too. How's your job?'

'No sign of Jake yet. When I rode up, I thought I'd found Tom's claim. I expected Jake to step out of that drift instead of you.'

'Sorry to disappoint you. Had your supper?'

'No. I'm out of grub. Aimed to ride back to Juniper and stock up.'

'I have to ride back and restock, myself. But there's enough left for one good meal for

46

the two of us. My camp's up the gully aways.'

They walked a hundred yards or so, passing two more of the tunnels.

Brad asked: 'Did Tom King have a claim around here?'

'Not that I know of. Tom never talked about his prospecting.'

'I thought maybe your man, Joe Hartwell, might have mentioned it.'

'No. Joe talked even less than Tom.'

'Where is he now?'

'On his way back East. I guess his share of the twenty thousand he took out looked pretty big to him after digging day wages for years.'

They angled up the bank and came out on a stony flat. A short distance away was a grove of trees and some grass.

'There's a spring over there,' Duke told Brad, pointing. 'That's my horse and jackass staked out over there. The camp's over here.'

Brad saw a lean-to built against a huge rock. Squares of sod had been laid atop the poles which slanted from the ground to the top of the boulder. It was open at both ends, and acted as a shelter for the supplies and equipment piled under it, as well as a place to sleep.

'You camp with me tonight,' Duke said, 'and we'll ride to Juniper tomorrow. Stake out your horse where mine is and fetch back some boughs to make a bed. I'll throw some grub together.'

Brad went about his chores, and when he came back, Duke had a campfire going and was cooking supper.

While they were eating, Duke said, 'I'll be glad of your company to town. I've taken out a pound or so of dust and nuggets this week, and I want to cash it in at the bank. If this fellow Jake has been snooping around, he might figure on holding me up. But he knows better than to tackle two of us.'

'Is your claim still in Hartwell's name?'

'No; he never filed on it. But after I cash in my gold, I'm going to ride to Sage City and file for myself. I have a hunch there's a lot more gold to be taken out, and I play my hunches.'

They turned in early, and after breakfast the next morning they prepared to start for Juniper.

'If you'll water and fetch in the horses,' said Duke, 'I'll straighten up camp.'

Brad set off toward the spring, and Duke went to a stone set against the boulder, rolled it aside, and took some sacks of gold from the hole he had uncovered. He had lied to Brad about what he had taken from the claim, for he did not want Brad to know how rich the claim really was. He had about five pounds of dust and nuggets in canvas sacks, and he poured all but a pound of it into his saddlebags.

48

Brad came in with the horses and the mule, and they rigged the animals there at the lean-to. Duke tied the canvas sack containing the pound of gold to his saddle horn, then slung on the saddlebags, handling them so that their weight was concealed from Brad.

They rode into Juniper that afternoon, and while Brad went to the store to buy supplies, Duke carried the gold into the bank.

'Looks like you had a good hunch,' observed Phil Bronson as he weighed the gold. 'Over five pounds, and you took it out in a week.'

'You keep that under your hat,' warned Duke. 'I don't want a stampede into those hills yet. If I hear any mention of this, I'll know who talked.'

Bronson tightened his lips and gave him a reproving look. 'I don't talk about the bank's business. You ought to know that, Duke.'

'Take out enough to pay off that note of mine,' Duke said, 'and give me the rest in cash. I'm riding to Sage tomorrow to file on the claim, and I want to order material. I'm going to hire men, build quarters for them, and go at this on a big scale.'

He took the money Bronson handed him and went to the hotel. He bathed, shaved, and changed into his neat and fashionable clothing. The role of prospector, even a successful one, did not appeal to him. In the future he'd confine himself to supervising the

49

work.

Except for one thing, he was content. That one thing kept popping up to disturb him. He had lost Tom King's letter to his daughter Judith in which Tom had accounted his big strike. Where or how he had lost it, he had no idea; it was missing when, after a day's furious digging at the mine, he had remembered the old location notice and the letter he carried in his pocket. The notice was still there, but the letter was gone. A thorough search of every place he had been proved fruitless.

Of one thing he was sure: the letter had been in his pocket when he left Juniper. Just to be positive, he went over his room carefully, searching everywhere. But he did not find the letter.

The loss had disturbed him greatly at first, but with the passage of the days his apprehension had worn off. Being a gambler, he took bad luck in stride. After all, the letter would tell the finder only that Tom had written his daughter about his big strike. No hint of the mine's location was given, and nobody could prove that the one Duke was working was the one Tom had found. It would be assumed that Tom himself had lost the letter. No, there was really nothing to fear.

He spent the evening at the Happy Chance, checking with Ed Carney, smiling at the jokes aimed at him as a prospector. He admitted he was green at it. Yes, he had found some color, nothing to get excited about, but he was satisfied that gold was there. At any rate, he was having fun and enjoying a little outdoor life.

He went to bed early, and the next morning set out for Sage City to file his claim.

★   ★   ★

Brad set out for the hills that same morning. Sheriff Rutherford had not visited Juniper during his absence, nor had he sent any word. That meant that Jake had made no attempt as yet to file on Tom's claim. Inquiry revealed that Jake had not been in Juniper.

The new deputy headed directly for Duke Fisher's claim because it was the one place he had come across where gold had recently been found. Somewhere along that dry creek bed he hoped to find Tom King's claim. The fact that Duke's friend, Joe Hartwell, had not mentioned Tom did not mean a thing; in this rugged country two men might live within a mile of each other and each be unaware of the other's presence. Another fact which caused him to return was that the creek bed was just about a half-day's ride from the boulder-strewn place of ambush.

He rode steadily, munching dry rations in the saddle, and it was around four in the afternoon when he reached the creek bed at Duke's claim. He turned into the draw, removing his hat and wiping his forehead with his scarf. He turned into the path which angled up the bank, intending to camp for the night under Duke's lean-to. He reached the top of the bank, started toward the camp, then pulled to a sudden halt.

The sun had moved behind the huge boulder forming a side of the lean-to, and the shadows beneath its roof were deep. Movement among these shadows caught Brad's attention. Some animal, probably a bear, must be prowling among the camp equipment. Then the crouching figure straightened.

It was a big-framed man who snatched a rifle and leaped out into the light. He was dressed in miner's clothing and wore a heavy black beard and mustache. He knew instantly it was the man for whom he had been searching, the claim-jumping killer called Jake.

The rifle snapped into line and, as it cracked, Brad threw himself from his horse. He heard the sound of the bullet as he was falling, and the next instant landed hard on his left side and started to roll.

An agonizing pain in his left thigh told him that he had struck his hip on a stone. The whole leg went numb. He stopped rolling, pushed himself to an elbow as Jake levered in another cartridge. Brad snatched out his Colt and fired. The bullet ricocheted from a stone, and Jake instinctively ducked. At once, Brad struggled to his feet and charged in a series of long hops. The rifle came up, and he made a desperate leap to his left. The bullet scratched his left shoulder. In his haste to reload, Jake jammed the rifle, and as Brad fired again, Jake ran inside the lean-to and through it. He dodged behind the boulder and was out of Brad's sight.

Brad hopped on, urgency driving him. This was the man who logically had killed Tom King; let him escape this time, and the odds were against finding him again. He heard the rattle of hoofs beyond the boulder when he was still fifty yards from the lean-to, and knew he'd need a horse to catch Jake.

He turned and hopped toward his horse, which stood over hanging reins where Brad had left him. The unnatural gait made the horse wary; it trotted a short distance and stopped.

Brad swore and stopped. He tried putting his weight on the injured leg, but it was pure agony. He gritted his teeth and tried to walk naturally, pain stabbing him at every step. The horse watched alertly but permitted him to grasp the bit. He lifted himself into the saddle and sped toward the lean-to. By the time he had rounded the boulder, Jake was out of sight. His tracks led along the creek bed.

Brad followed and when he reached the gully, found that a bend hid Jake from view. He sent his horse racing along the dry bed, holding the rifle ready for a quick shot. He rounded the bend and pulled up to listen. Far to his left he heard hoofbeats; Jake had cut into a lateral passage and was in the hills.

For the rest of the afternoon Brad searched without success. With the coming of darkness, he was discouraged; Jake was warned now and would be on guard every moment. He might even leave that section of the country altogether.

Brad spent the night under the lean-to, and the next morning started back toward Juniper and Sage, to report to Sheriff Rutherford.

CHAPTER SIX

He rode into Juniper that afternoon, following the weekly stage from Briscoe. When he put his horse in the jail stable, he found Rutherford's horse there. The sheriff was somewhere in town; Brad found him at the Happy Chance.

'He was in Duke's lean-to when I spotted him,' Brad said, recounting the events of the last two days. 'I found that some stones had been moved where he was looking for gold.'

54

'He must have been spying on Duke as he spied on Tom.'

'Yeah. But if he murdered Tom to get his claim, why isn't he working it instead of trying to steal from Duke?'

'Jake would rather let another fellow dig it, then take it.'

'I guess Jake hasn't tried to file yet.'

'No. Duke Fisher located on a claim yesterday afternoon. That's one of the reasons I rode to Juniper; I didn't know you already knew that Duke had turned prospector.'

'He claims that he grubstaked a miner named Joe Hartwell, that Joe took out twenty thousand, split with Duke, and started for home back East. Did you know this Joe Hartwell?'

'I've seen him around, but not within the last month or so.' He gave Brad a quick glance. 'Are you figuring that Duke might have stumbled on Tom's claim?'

'It's a possibility. If Duke's lying about Hartwell, it's even possible that he murdered Tom. But you say there actually is such a man, and that backs up his story. Anyhow, I'd like to check on Duke the night Tom was killed.'

'We'll do that, of course; but Duke has money. Why would he murder anybody for a mining claim? Well, let's go up to the hotel and ask Harry a few questions.'

On the way to the hotel Brad said, 'I know

Duke went with Tom to the livery corral that night to get a horse for him, and I know that Duke was at the hotel early the next morning, if Harry told the truth. Where he was during the night is the thing to find out.'

They found Harry wandering listlessly around with a dust cloth in his hand. 'You want rooms?' he asked hopefully.

'Information,' answered Rutherford. 'I want to know who stayed at the hotel the night Tom King was murdered.'

Harry opened the register. 'What date was it?'

When Rutherford told him, Harry ran his finger along the names. 'Here it is. Only one guest, and that was Hollister here. That's all.'

'Were you still up when Duke came back from the Happy Chance?'

'He didn't go to the Happy Chance that night. He went with Tom to the corral, then came back and said he wasn't feeling good and was going right to bed. He went upstairs and didn't come down until next morning.'

'Sure of that?'

'Sure, I'm sure. There's only one set of stairs, and I sleep in that room right off them. I would have heard him if he'd come down that night. Say, you trying to pin that killing on Duke? You're crazy!'

'Just checking,' said Rutherford. 'Checking everybody.'

'Even if Duke sneaked down later, I was

56

up until after midnight, and by that time Tom would have been too far ahead to catch before he got to Sage.'

'That lets Duke out,' said the sheriff when they left the hotel. 'I just can't see Duke as Tom's killer. For one thing, he don't carry a rope. I doubt if he could put a loop over a fence post standing five feet away.'

'That brings us back to Jake. John, you still want me as deputy?'

'I do. Until you round up Jake or get sick of the job.'

'O.K. He'll be on guard every minute, but I'll get him. He came near to killing me, and my hip's still sore as a boil.'

They ate an early supper at the restaurant, and the sheriff set out for Sage City. Brad spent the night on the cot, and next morning headed again for Duke's claim.

For the next ten days he searched determinedly. He found no trace of Jake. He explored the dry creek for its full length, found some worthless abandoned workings. It seemed that Duke had filed on the only worthwhile claim in that part of the country.

Once more his supplies ran out, but now he was nearer to Briscoe than to Juniper, and he decided to replenish them at the former town. He spent a night at the Briscoe House, asked questions, but got no satisfactory answers. Nobody seemed to know Jake, although several recalled big, black bearded miners answering his description. One of these had bought supplies just two days before. It could have been Jake, although again he was reminded that there were many black-bearded miners of Jake's build.

He decided to return to the vicinity of Duke's claim. Jake's specialty now seemed to be gold robbery, and here gold was being taken out of the rocky ground. Brad decided to camp near the mine and keep out of sight in the hope that Jake would come back. It seemed to be his best chance.

He found the mine a beehive of activity. Duke had hired a half-dozen men; lumber had been freighted in and a bunkhouse built. Two of the men were now constructing a mess hall. When Brad asked for Duke, one of the men directed him to a small office at one end of the bunkhouse.

Duke was no longer dressed as a miner. Now his hair was carefully combed and his mustache freshly waxed and pointed. He greeted Brad indifferently. 'No luck, I suppose?'

'No. Did Rutherford tell you about my finding Jake at your camp?'

'No, he didn't.' Duke frowned. 'So that's who messed things up for me. I found some stones moved around. It's a good thing I took the gold to Juniper that day. Well, he won't try it again—too many men around.'

'How is the claim panning out?'

'Just as my hunch told me it would. We uncovered a vein and followed it, and there's no sign of it pinching out.'

'Kind of funny Joe Hartwell didn't find it, isn't it?'

'If he had gone just a little farther he would have; but he was anxious to get back East. Got a wife there, and ten thousand dollars looked pretty big to him.' He smiled thinly. 'I'm glad he didn't find it.'

'I can't figure out where Tom King had his claim. When I found this dry creek bed and Jake hanging around it, I was sure it was somewhere around here.'

'I'm beginning to doubt that Tom had a claim,' said Duke. 'You and John are just assuming that the reason Tom wanted to go to Sage in such a hurry was to file; it might have been something quite different.'

'Like what?'

'He had a thousand dollars on him. Maybe he was anxious to get it to his daughter.'

'Why did Jake try to kill him if it wasn't to keep him from filing?'

Duke shrugged. 'There may have been a personal quarrel between them. Sure, he never said anything to you about it, but Tom always was close-mouthed. It seems that if he had found a rich claim, you would have come across it by this time. You've been looking for it—how long? About three weeks. Still a deputy sheriff?'

'Yes.'

'Then I have something useful for you to do. Much of what we're taking out of the mine is ore that has to go to a stamping mill; but there's a lot of dust and nuggets that I can ship through the bank at Juniper. The stage comes through on Saturday, and I've made arrangements to have it picked up; but we'll have to transport it to the Briscoe-Juniper road. It's pretty rough country, and with this guy Jake on the loose, I think it would be a good idea for you to act as guard when we move it.

'There'll be two on the seat of the buckboard I'm using, and if you'll ride on ahead and make sure nobody is lying in wait for the shipment, I can fetch up in the rear.'

'How much gold are you shipping?'

'Around five thousand dollars' worth. Won't weight over twenty pounds, box and all, and one man could handle it easy. Jake's just the man to try it. For all I know, he might be watching the mine right now. I thought you might want to go along just on the chance that he does try a holdup. You'd have him then, dead to rights.'

'All right, I'll go along—and hope he does make a try at it. That will be Saturday morning?'

'Right. Day after tomorrow.'

Brad left the mine and scouted around, looking for sign of Jake. He found nothing.

He camped near the mine and all day Friday continued his cautious search, but his labors were in vain. He turned in on Friday night with a feeling of discouragement. Perhaps Duke was right; perhaps Tom had not found a rich claim at all.

It was time, he thought, that he get busy locating on that cattle ranch. He determined to get Judith King's address from Rutherford and write her about the homestead. While awaiting her answer, he would look around for a good cattle buy.

The next morning he reported at the mine. Duke had had a sturdy oak box fitted with a strong lock, and in this he had put the dust and nuggets he intended to ship to Juniper. The box was placed in the buckboard, and two men mounted to the seat. Brad started off, the buckboard following him and Duke riding a hundred yards in its rear.

Brad ranged back and forth on both sides of the road, but he saw no sign of Jake, and the whole party reached the Briscoe-Juniper road around ten o'clock. The stagecoach arrived an hour later, and while the gold was put aboard, its three passengers got out to stretch their legs.

The first was a short, stout man dressed in the best Eastern fashion. Brad guessed he was a salesman of some kind. This man turned and gave a hand to a second passenger, a prim, severely dressed, middle-aged woman who might have been a schoolteacher or milliner.

The third passenger was a very lovely young lady, and Brad was struck at once by the sharp contrast between her somber black bonnet and the blonde hair and lively blue eyes beneath it. She wore a black traveling suit and held a small beaded bag.

She gave the stout man a brief smile of thanks for his help, then her gaze fell on Duke Fisher, and Brad saw the light of recognition come into her face. She came quickly toward them.

'Excuse me,' she said to Duke, 'but you're Mr. Fisher, aren't you?'

Duke took off his hat. 'That's correct, Miss. I'm sorry; I don't seem—'

'Of course you don't remember me. I was just a little girl when you last saw me. I'm Judith King.'

'Tom's daughter! I remember you now. This is Brad Hollister, Sheriff Rutherford's deputy. Rutherford wrote you, didn't he?'

Brad tipped his hat, and she gave him a brief, impersonal smile.

'If he did, I left before the letter arrived. He sent me a telegram saying my father had a fatal accident and that he'd write details later. I left at once. Mr. Fisher, what happened to my father?'

'He was shot, Miss King.'

'Who—who shot him?'

'A miner known only as Jake. Rutherford and Hollister have been searching for him ever since.'

'But why? Why did he kill father?'

'We don't know. A personal quarrel, probably.'

The driver called, 'All aboard!' then, and Duke turned to Brad. 'I'm going to ride in the coach with Miss King. She'll have questions to ask, I'm sure. Tie my horse to the back of the stage, will you? And thanks for your help.'

Brad took the rein and moved with the horse to the back of the stage. He tied the animal; the stage moved off; and he stood looking after it. The two men in the buckboard yelled a good-by, which he mechanically answered.

After a moment, he got into his saddle and set out in the wake of the stage.

CHAPTER SEVEN

Duke Fisher and Judith King sat on the rear seat of the stage, while the fat man and the spinster occupied the one in front of them. The girl spoke first.

'Tell me about father.'

He told her of the first ambush.

'It happened on this road. I'll point out the

place when we come to it.' Then Duke told Judith King about Jake's ambushing her father, about Brad's intervention, and then of Tom King's bullet-riddled body having been found by Sheriff Rutherford on the Sage City road, next day.

'It was this man Jake who did it? You're sure?'

'Who else could it have been? Jake had tried to kill him earlier, but Hollister drove him off. Riding double that way, Brad and Tom couldn't make much time, and Jake probably cut around them and waited for your father.'

'Why,' she asked, 'was father so anxious to get to Sage City? Why did he ride on that night instead of waiting until the next day?'

'The sheriff is working on the theory that Tom had made a rich gold strike and was hurrying to Sage to file on the claim. They think Jake found out he had struck it rich, then killed him to get the claim himself.' At that point, Duke asked the question that was so important to him: 'Had your father mentioned any such strike to you?'

She shook her head. 'No. He sent me money every month, but he never said where he got it. I thought he just moved about from place to place taking a little here, a little there.'

'But he said nothing about finding a rich claim?'

'Nothing. Oh, he kept telling me that when he did make the strike, the first thing he would do was send for me so that we could be together again. He always said that.'

Duke relaxed. So she knew nothing whatever about Tom's rich strike. He was safe, perfectly safe.

After a short silence Duke said, 'I'm surprised that you came out here. Now that your father is gone, you'll be alone.'

'I was born out here, Mr Fisher, and I've never really gotten used to cities. I looked forward to the time when I could return to the West.'

'What will you do? Have you made any plans?'

'Lots of plans. The homestead on the Bitterroot is mine; I'm going to try my hand at raising poultry.'

'Poultry?'

'Yes. Fresh eggs are scarce out here, and a stuffed chicken for Sunday dinner will be a welcome change from beef. Don't you think so?'

He nodded. 'Yes, I do. But it will be mighty lonesome out there.'

'I expect to be too busy to be lonesome. After I get my poultry started I'll buy a couple of good milk cows. I can make butter and sell it in Juniper.' She gave him a quiet smile. 'Oh, I have lots of plans.'

They rode for a short while in silence; then

he pointed through the window. 'This is the place where Jake ambushed your father the first time. He was circling to get a clean shot at Tom when Hollister arrived and scared him off.'

She kept her gaze on the place until the coach had passed, then sank back in the seat with a little sigh. 'I must thank Mr. Hollister for saving father.'

'He may run across Jake yet. I pity the man if he does.'

'I think he and the sheriff are wrong about father's having found a rich claim,' she said. 'He would have written about it if he had. Mr. Rutherford sent me a thousand dollars that was father's. He must have been riding to Sage City to telegraph some of it to me. He was very punctual about sending money to me, but I had not heard from him for five weeks, and I had almost run out of cash.'

They heard the driver shout, heard the grate of the brake. The coach swerved to the side of the road and stopped. Judith put her head out the window. The guard was climbing down from the box.

'What is it?' she asked.

He spoke without turning his head. 'Man's layin' in the middle of the road. Looks like he's dead.'

The coach had just rounded a curve which ran along the base of a huge boulder, and the man in the road had not been seen until they

66

were quite close to him. He was lying face down, arms outflung, legs drawn up.

The guard prodded the shape tentatively with a boot toe, then bent over, grasped the man by a shoulder and rolled him over on his back. All that Judith could distinguish of the features was a heavy black beard.

The supposedly dead man suddenly came alive. A hand shot up and fastened on the shotgun barrel and gave a violent jerk. The guard was yanked off balance and fell over the other. Instantly the bearded man rolled and got to his knees astride the guard. Judith saw the man's revolver barrel rise and come down on the head of the guard. He went limp.

The man came to his feet and wheeled with the speed of a cat, the Colt level. He strode toward the coach, and his gaze was fixed on Judith's face. He halted opposite the lead team.

'You people in the coach come out!' he grated. 'On this side, one at a time, and no monkey business. You first, lady.'

'What is it?' asked the fat bald-headed man, turning to look at Judith.

'A holdup,' said Judith tightly. 'We'd better do as he tells us.'

She heard Duke Fisher swear. Clutching the beaded bag firmly, she opened the door and got out. Duke followed her.

'Hands in the air, mister!'

Duke glared, then slowly raised his hands.

'Go over there and stand with your faces to the rock.'

They crossed the road and did as directed.

The bandit strode to where the four stood. He jerked Duke's gun from its holster and flung it under the coach, then felt him over for other weapons. He took a short-barreled revolver from the fat man's pocket and tossed it after Duke's Colt. He turned and spoke to the driver.

'Wrap the lines around the brake lever and throw down that box.'

The driver did so, the box hitting the road with a dull thump.

'Now, lady,' the bandit said to Judith, 'you can turn around and hand over your money.'

With her free hand, she took a change purse from her pocket and handed it to him. He opened it and glanced at its contents.

'Chicken feed. Where's the rest of it?'

'That's all there is.'

'You're better heeled than that. What you got in the other hand?' He seized her arm, jerked the hand from behind her back. He tore the beaded bag from her hand.

'Please!' she begged. 'It's all I have!'

'It's all you *had*,' he corrected and thrust the bag into a pocket.

He stiffened suddenly, listening. Judith saw his face go tense and listened also. From beyond the curve and out of their sight came the unmistakable beat of hoofs.

The bandit glanced quickly at the box lying in the road, ran to it, raised it. Then he dropped it, realizing that he could not make the trip to his hidden horse before the rider came into sight.

'You four, circle around this end of the rock,' he ordered. 'Keep your faces to it and your hands in sight. Move!'

When they did so, and would be out of sight of the approaching horseman, the bandit said to the driver, 'You sit tight. Don't turn and don't try to warn this feller, or I'll drop you.'

He moved in front of the lead team, where he could see the rider as he rounded the curve and at the same time keep the driver and four passengers under observation.

Comprehension of what he intended to do reached Judith. The rider would round the boulder, see the stage at a halt, and would pull up. The bandit, concealed from his sight by the horses, would shoot him. He had to; the box of gold was there in the road, and he would not leave it. She turned her head and saw the bandit, crouching, peering toward the point where the rider would come into sight. He held his Colt ready to throw down.

She acted almost instinctively, without regarding consequences. Like a frightened road runner, she raced around the rock to her right. Half a dozen strides would take her out of the bandit's sight, and he would not fire at once for fear of warning the approaching rider. She heard the bandit call out, cursing her, but there was no shot, and a hasty glance over her shoulder showed her only the rounded surface of the rock. She was out of danger.

She had to reach the road beyond the curve. She dodged around rocks, had a glimpse of the approaching horseman, waved her arms and shouted before leaping to the ground and running some more. She came out into the road and almost under the feet of the prancing horse. In her excitement she did not at first recognize Brad Hollister.

'Holdup!' she panted. 'Just around the curve! He's hiding—in front—horses! Going to shoot you! Stay away!'

He slipped from the saddle, thrust the rein into her hand.

'Hold the horse for me. If things go wrong, ride out of here.'

He turned and ran to the big boulder, drawing his gun, and suddenly she recognized him as the man Duke Fisher had introduced, the man who had saved her father.

Brad edged carefully around the boulder. He saw the stagecoach standing at the side of the road, saw the blackbearded face over the back of the near lead horse, saw the movement of the six gun as it came down to cover him. He pulled back as the weapon roared and chips flew from the rock. He leaped out into the road, snapped a shot, holding high to avoid hitting a horse.

The bandit turned and ran, keeping the horses between him and Brad for fifty feet or so, then darted across the road toward the rocks on the far side. Brad fired two more quick shots, but both missed. He ran in pursuit.

He noticed the guard lying in the road, the three people standing against the boulder, and then the box beside the coach. But at the time, all that registered with him was the blackbearded bandit—Jake.

Brad reached the rocks among which Jake had vanished. He heard the sudden rattle of hoofs and had a brief glimpse of the mounted Jake as he flashed past an opening and then disappeared. Brad ran back, passing the stage without stopping. Duke Fisher was standing over the specie box, and the other two passengers were beside him. The driver had come down from the box and was ministering to the guard.

Judith King stood where he had left her. He took the rein and answered her unspoken question. 'He got away.'

She moved away from him, her arms extended like a blind person. She sank down on a stone. She made no sound, but there were tears in her eyes.

He moved quickly over to her. 'What's the

71

matter, Miss King? Did he hurt you?'

She shook her head. 'No, no. W-worse than that. He took my purse. There were six hundred-dollar bills in it. It's pretty nearly all I have in the world!'

She was looking appealingly up at him, and even in her distress she was the prettiest woman he had ever seen. A great pity stirred him as he considered the plight in which she found herself: her father murdered, alone in a country that was still predominantly male, without money or friends.

'I'll get that money back for you, Miss King. Believe me, I will,' he said.

He saw hope come into her eyes, her face light up. She sprang up, put both hands on his arms, clutched them tightly. 'Mr. Hollister, *can* you?'

'I'll get it back. That's a promise.'

He really meant it. He stepped into the saddle and rode away, leaving her standing there.

CHAPTER EIGHT

The stage resumed its journey, the box of gold once more aboard it. The fat bald-headed man was smugly complacent, his stuffed wallet still secure in his pocket; the spinster sat primly upright, thankful that they

72

all had not been murdered; Duke Fisher, face impassive, was assured that his luck still held.

Only Judith was dejected. The six hundred-dollar bills had been carefully hoarded for the purpose of starting her poultry farm, and now they were gone and there remained in her change purse only enough to pay for a few nights' lodging and a few frugal meals.

Brad Hollister had promised he would get the money back for her, but to do that he must capture the bandit, and it sometimes took months to capture an outlaw. She got off the stage at Juniper with the deepest feeling of hopelessness she had ever experienced.

Duke hurried at once to the bank with his precious box, and Harry, the hotel clerk, carried Judith King's small trunk and valise into the lobby. The fat man had a heavy valise which he carried himself.

'You both want rooms, I reckon. Sign the register.'

The fat man wrote his name in the book, and Harry gave him a key.

'Number's on the door; you won't have any trouble finding it.'

The fat man said, 'I'm looking for a gentleman named Duke Fisher.'

'He was riding the same stage with you. Right now he's down at the bank.'

'Is that so? Dark-haired gentleman with a waxed mustache?'

73

'That's him. He lives right here at the hotel. Owns it.'

'Please tell him I'd like to talk with him at his earliest opportunity.'

Judith signed her name beneath the fat man's. She noticed that he had signed his as T. Jefferson Mason.

Harry shouldered her trunk and carried it upstairs, and Judith followed him with her valise. She thanked him listlessly and he went out, closing the door behind him. For a while she stood looking about her. Her surroundings were drab, but clean. A bed, a dresser, a washstand, two chairs. One window, fairly clean. She went to it and looked into the street.

Across from the hotel was a general store with a bench outside the open doorway. Beside the store was a harness shop, and farther along the street she saw a barber pole. On the other side of the store was a saloon, and on the corner beyond that, a small building with bronze letters spelling *Cattlemen's Bank*. There were a couple of houses, and beyond them she could not see. Just a dusty, gray little cowtown, its one street lined with hitching posts and long rails. There would be no jobs in Juniper for a young woman unless the storekeeper needed a clerk. She could not mend harness or make saddles; she could not shave men or cut their hair; she knew nothing about office work even if the bank would consider hiring an unknown young woman.

She turned away from the window, her face tight and her fists clenched. Her only hope lay in Brad Hollister. He must get her six hundred dollars back—he must!

★　　★　　★

Duke Fisher came back from the bank, and Harry told him that the man who had signed himself T. Jefferson Mason wanted to see him.

'He's the fat tenderfoot who came in on the stage with you.'

'Probably wants to sell me something.'

'He didn't say. I put him in Number Two.'

Duke went upstairs, knocked on the door, and was told to come in. The fat man was unpacking his valise and turned when Duke entered.

'I'm Duke Fisher. The clerk said you wanted to see me.'

'Yes. Permit me to introduce myself.' He took out a leather case, extracted two cards and a folded letter. He handed them to Duke and said, 'Please sit down, sir.'

Duke sat down, looked at the cards. One bore the engraved name, *T. Jefferson Mason*, and beneath that were two lines reading, *Field Engineer, Atchison, Topeka and Santa Fe Railroad*. The other was a pass issued to T.

Jefferson Mason good on all divisions of the road. Duke unfolded the letter.

It informed anyone whom it might concern that the bearer, T. Jefferson Mason, was an agent of the company, and requested the full cooperation of those he might contact on company business. The letter was written on company stationery and had the name of the president at its bottom.

Duke refolded the letter and handed it and the cards back to Mason.

'So you're T. Jefferson Mason, field engineer for the Atchison, Topeka and Santa Fe. What about it?'

'You may have heard a rumor that the company is going to extend its lines into this part of the country.'

'No, I hadn't heard it.'

'I'm surprised. News of that kind generally gets around. Well, there is such a rumor, and if it is correct, the man who knows in advance where the railroad will run can make a fortune.'

He seated himself in another chair, offered a case of cigars to Duke, who refused, lighted one himself.

'How would this fortune be acquired?' asked Duke.

The fat man raised his eyebrows 'My dear sir, land along a railroad right-of-way increases in value by leaps and bounds, especially that which is adjacent to a railway

76

station. I understand that you own quite a bit of property in Juniper; if you knew that the railroad was going to pass through this town, you could acquire as much more as possible, at a low figure, and later sell at an enormous profit.'

'Are you telling me the road is coming through Juniper?'

'I'm telling you nothing; I am simply pointing out possibilities. If the road runs through this town, your fortune is made, for a railroad station would immediately be built, and Juniper, as a shipping center, would blossom like the rose. On the other hand, if the road passes elsewhere through this basin, a new town would spring up around the station and your holdings here would become worthless.'

Duke's eyes narrowed slightly. 'What's the cure for that?'

Mason smiled. 'The remedy would be to unload all you have in Juniper and buy all you can at the location of the new town. Always provided that you knew in advance just where this new town would spring up, and that you bought before that knowledge became common. Once it becomes known that the road is coming in, you would have to pay enormous prices for land, if you were able to buy at all.'

Duke was studying Mason, his face showing none of the excitement which was beginning to grip him. 'If the line comes in, it would logically run through Juniper. The town is already established.'

'The Atchison, Topeka and Santa Fe has no interest whatever in Juniper. A town will grow wherever that station is built. Several routes have been considered. One would run through this town; the others would miss it by from ten to fifty miles. Wouldn't you like to know, Mr. Fisher, just which route will be followed?'

'I suppose you know,' said Duke drily, sensing some kind of con game.

'I know exactly where the line will run. As a matter of fact, I have been sent there by the company to make the final decision, and a crew is awaiting my order to begin the survey. Once that crew comes into this basin the whole country will know where the line is to run, and there will be a scramble to buy along the right-of-way. Naturally, land prices will skyrocket; but the one who knows in advance will be able to buy desirable acreage for a song. I am prepared to sell that information to any man who is farsighted enough to realize the enormous profits which will accrue to him.'

Duke's eyes were cold. 'Nothing doing, Mason. If you had this information you'd use it yourself instead of trying to peddle it to the first sucker you come across.'

Mason tightened his full lips. 'Very well,

Mr. Fisher. I hope I haven't taken too much of your time. When can I get a stage to Sage City?'

'There won't be another for a week.'

'Then I will have to hire somebody to drive me to Sage City. Do you know anyone I can get?'

'I own a livery corral, and I can find a man to drive you.' He regarded Mason thoughtfully. 'Look here; if you can give me one good reason for selling this information instead of using it yourself, I might be interested.'

'It's very simple. For one thing, if I took advantage of this confidential knowledge myself, I would forfeit a very excellent position with the company and be blacklisted so that I'd never get another one as good. But that alone would not stop me, because the enormous profit to be realized would compensate for a dozen such jobs. The real reason is that I haven't the capital to swing such a deal. We've been through a panic, Mr. Fisher, in which I lost not only my shirt but my pants as well. I was deeply involved in the stock market, and I tried to hold on. I mortgaged everything I owned and borrowed all I could. When they finally sold me out, I was not only broke but also deeply in debt. I earn a very satisfactory salary, but it takes every penny I earn to keep my creditors fairly well satisfied and maintain my family. Selling

79

this information is the only hope I have of getting back on my feet. What I get I will invest farther along the line and in such a way that the company will not find it out at once. It's the best that I can do.'

He fixed Duke with an angry stare. 'Do you think I'd be fool enough to share this knowledge with anybody if I had any capital at all?'

'What's your price?'

'Ten thousand dollars, cash.'

Duke considered. He could understand Mason's position, for he had passed through the same painful experience during the panic. Before his 'discovery' of the mine, if somebody had offered the U.S. mint and all its contents for a thousand dollars, he would have been unable to buy it.

'I'm not fool enough to pay you a cent until you give me proof that you know where the line is coming in.'

'And I'm not fool enough to tell you where it's coming in until I have the ten thousand. I think, Mr. Fisher, we're both wasting time. Can you have me driven to Sage City in the morning?'

Duke waved this aside. 'If I did pay you ten thousand dollars, how soon will I have proof that the line is coming in where you say it is?'

'The surveying crew should reach the basin in about two weeks. After that, it will be another week before it is definitely known where the line will run. Options on the land should be taken before the crew enters this basin. That's why I'm anxious to close this business without delay.'

Duke considered a moment longer.

'I'll buy it,' he announced, 'on one condition. You stay right here in Juniper with that ten thousand until the surveyors come in.'

'I was prepared to do that in any event. No man with any sense would let another walk off with ten thousand dollars without first being assured that he was not being swindled. I must leave Juniper only long enough to drive to Sage City and telegraph the crew to start the survey. You may accompany me if you wish.'

'I'll do that. Now, where is the road to run?'

Mason shook his head, smiled gently. 'The money first, Mr. Fisher. I trust you no farther than you trust me.'

Duke shrugged, looked at his watch. 'The bank is closed. It will have to wait until morning. It will be Sunday, but I can get the money.'

They got up, and Mason stepped past Duke and opened the door for him.

Duke walked to the restaurant for his supper, reviewing the conversation as he walked. He searched for a catch somewhere

81

but could find none. His ten thousand would be in no jeopardy, for he could keep Mason under surveillance every minute of the day and night. Mason would not be permitted to mail a letter without its first being read; he would be given no opportunity to send the money out by stage. He would be watched until the surveyors actually were in the basin. The ten thousand would be safe, and Mason must know it.

He contemplated the future while he ate. The possibilities were unlimited. If the line was to pass through Juniper, he would buy up everything he could get. It would be easy, for men were in need of money. If the road went elsewhere, he would dispose of his Juniper property, taking whatever he could get, and would buy along the proposed right-of-way. If he owned the land upon which the new station was to be built, he could easily become a millionaire in time, for the new town would grow and keep growing.

He expanded. With a rich gold mine pouring its wealth in his lap, and real estate which multiplied in value as the town grew, he would become one of the wealthiest men in the West.

The next morning Duke went to Phil Bronson's house. 'Phil,' he said, 'yesterday I deposited something like five thousand with you. There will be more where that came from. Right now, I must have ten thousand to close a deal. Let me have it for thirty days. All my property is clear now, and I'll pay you with gold from the mine within that time.'

'Be glad to let you have the money, Duke. Just give me your personal note for the amount.'

They went to the bank, and Phil opened the vault and gave Duke the ten thousand. Duke executed a thirty-day note and returned to the hotel with the cash. T. Jefferson Mason was seated in the lobby scanning a newspaper. Duke motioned to him and led the way upstairs.

'In my room, if you please,' said Mason. 'There is something I must show you when the deal is closed.'

They went into Mason's room, and he bolted the door behind them. Duke handed him the bills and said, 'Count it.' After Mason did so, Duke said, 'Now tell me where that railroad will run.'

Mason lifted his valise to the bed, opened it, took out a roll of drafting paper. He spread it out, and Duke recognized a map of the basin. There were four red lines crossing it, marked A, B, C, and D.

'These are the four routes which were considered,' explained Mason. 'As you see, Route B runs through Juniper.'

'I see it. I also see that it's the most direct route. Mason, you've foxed me; the road is coming through Juniper after all.'

'Even if it were, it would be worth the ten thousand to know it. But you're wrong; the road is not coming through Juniper. I eliminated it for one very good reason. Juniper depends on wells for its water supply, and in the dry season the wells often go dry. I understand that on occasion you have to haul water all the way from the Bitterroot.'

'What has that got to do with it?'

'A lot. Steam engines must have water in order to run, and they must fill their tanks along the right-of-way. The new road will run along the route marked A, generally following the Bitterroot River, where water will be accessible. It will run along the east bank because in many places the hills come clear to the water on the west side.' He put a finger on the map. 'Here a spring gushes out of the hills, which, because of its height, will feed water to the tank by gravity, thus making the use of a pump unnecessary.'

Duke nodded. He knew that spring; it was directly across the Bitterroot from the King homestead.

'The station,' Mason went on, 'will be erected on one side or the other of this spring. A new town will grow up around it.' He gave Duke a grave look. 'You will be glad, Mr. Fisher, that you bought this information from me. Juniper is doomed as a town of any consequence. You must dispose of your holdings and invest everything you have in

84

land along the Bitterroot, especially where the new town will be located.'

Duke thought swiftly. The homestead now belonged to Judith King, and Judith King had just been robbed of six hundred dollars, and she could not have much money left. He should be able to buy that land from her without any trouble.

'Let's go down to the Happy Chance and have a drink,' he said.

'Gladly. After that you must drive me to Sage City. I must get word to my crew. I suppose the telegraph office is open on Sunday?'

They walked to the Happy Chance and had their drink. Duke called a thin-featured, hard-faced man from the faro table to share the drink with them.

'Quant,' he said, 'this is Mr. Mason. Mason, meet Quant.'

'Hyuh,' said Quant.

'Delighted, I'm sure,' said Mason.

'From here on,' said Duke, 'you two are going to be inseparable pals. Quant, you'll share his room at the hotel and go with him wherever he goes. He has the freedom of the town, but you're to see to it that he mails no letters without my reading them first or sends any package through the mail or by stage or messenger. You can pick out a man to spell you, but I'm holding you responsible. You'll eat at the restaurant. Mason will pay for his meals, but you can charge yours to me. Got it?'

'Got it.'

'Good. Now trot down to the corral and hitch up a buckboard. Mr. Mason and I are driving to Sage, and you'll go along on horseback.'

Quant tossed off his drink and left, and they followed him shortly afterward. They drove to Sage City and Mason sent a telegram. He let Duke read it. It said simply, 'Start Immediately Route A. Mason.'

They returned to Juniper that afternoon. The whole time Mason had been under close surveillance; they had driven directly to the telegraph office and Mason had been given no chance to dispose of the ten thousand dollars had he wished to.

This, Duke told himself, was not gambling. This time he was playing a sure thing.

CHAPTER NINE

Brad started his pursuit of Jake with the firm conviction that this time he would catch the man. Jake had only a short start, and the hard ground made hoofbeats audible and would indicate to Brad the direction Jake was taking.

But it did not work out that way; sounds of Jake's progress were drowned out by the noise made by Brad's own horse, and since Jake changed his course frequently, Brad had to stop often in order to listen. Each time he stopped he lost ground. Also, Brad was in unfamiliar country, for it had not been included in his long search. Once more the wily Jake had given him the slip.

Brad kept up the search until darkness came, then made a dry camp. He had promised Judith King he would get her six hundred dollars back, and he would keep that promise; but the search for Jake promised to become a long-drawn-out affair, and while he had some supplies left, the best plan would be to return to Juniper and restock. It was Sunday and the store would not be open, so there was no hurry in returning.

He came to the stage road around noon and rode into town that evening. He rode directly to the Elite Cafe and went into the restaurant for his supper. Judith King sat at one of the tables, and, half rising, looked at him expectantly. He sat down on the chair opposite her.

'I haven't caught him yet, but I will.'

The light went out of her face, but she managed to smile. 'I'm sure you will. I—I just hope it will be soon.'

The waiter came over to the table, and Brad looked at the bowl of soup before the girl. 'Have you ordered your supper?'

'This is it. I'm not at all hungry.'

'I guess not, after what happened. But you'll feel better with a good meal under your belt.' He said to the waiter, 'Bring us two steaks with all the trimmings.'

She opened her mouth to protest, but he gave her a grin as the waiter went into the kitchen.

'You don't have to eat if you don't want to,' he said, 'but you can keep me company. I want to talk to you.'

'I have something to tell you, too. Mr. Fisher said you saved my father that first time he was ambushed, and I want to thank you.'

'I should have shot Jake then and there. Trouble was, I didn't know either him or your father, didn't know who was right and who was wrong.'

'I know. I don't blame you. You saved him that first time; it wasn't your fault that you weren't on hand to save him the second time. Mr. Fisher said the sheriff made you a deputy and gave you the job of catching the man.'

'Yes. I met Rutherford in Kansas when I was a town marshal up there. He was looking for a killer, and I helped round him up. John had to let his deputies go when the panic hit, and this Jake needed catching, and I had just met and got to like your father, so—' He spread his hands and let it go at that.

'How did you happen to come down here?'

'That's what I want to talk to you about. The homestead on the Bitterroot—it's yours now?'

'Yes.'

'I've seen it, and it struck me right away as just the thing I'm looking for. I'd like to buy it from you.'

'Oh, I'm sorry. I planned to have a poultry farm out there; raise chickens and sell the eggs, and later on add a couple of cows and sell butter. I'm sure I can make a living at it. It's really why I came out here.'

He gave her another grin, then quickly suppressed it. 'That's a mighty good idea, Miss King. Eggs and butter are scarce and bring a good price. Funny, with all the cows running the range, so little butter is made. But then I guess you never tried milking a range cow.'

'Indeed I have! And got kicked nearly through the barn.'

'And got mighty little milk, I bet. But if you get a couple good Jerseys, you'll sure make a go of it. As for me, there's plenty of range for the taking. I just sort of hoped—' He let it trail off.

'I'm really sorry, Mr. Hollister. If I ever do sell and you haven't found anything to suit you, I'd rather you have the homestead than anybody I know.'

They talked more before their meal arrived, and they talked while they ate.

Before they had finished they were calling each other by their first names.

He walked with her to the hotel, and they sat on the veranda and talked still further. He sensed her need for money badly, but just how badly he did not guess.

Early the next morning Brad left Juniper with his supplies.

Judith spent all but a few cents of her money for breakfast. There was only one thing for her to do: that was to get a job. When she left the restaurant, she went directly to the store. The storekeeper, a hard-faced man of middle age who had just managed to survive the panic, was behind the counter.

'I'm Judith King,' she said. 'Perhaps you knew my father, Tom King.'

'Yes, Miss, I knew him. He used to trade with me.'

'I came here to settle on our homestead, but the stage was held up and I was robbed of practically all my money. I must find work of some kind, and was wondering if you could use me as a clerk.'

'Ma'am, I could use you right enough, but I can't afford to hire a clerk right now. During the panic I carried folks on the books and pretty near went bust myself. I'd like to help you, but I just can't.'

'Do you know anybody who has a job?'

He shook his head. 'No one in Juniper;

we're all in the same boat. You might try Phil Bronson at the bank. He used to keep a clerk when times were good.'

Judith went to the bank and talked to Phil Bronson. She had to confess, in answer to his questions, that she knew nothing about banking or bookkeeping. He shook his head sadly.

'My dear young lady, times have been hard and I have to handle everything myself. Even if I could afford it, I couldn't hire an inexperienced young woman when the man who used to work for me is waiting to get his job back. I'm sure you understand.'

Judith said that she did, but all she really understood was that she had to have a job, any kind of job, in a big hurry. She went to the restaurant and talked to its owner. She could wait on tables or behind the counter; she could cook; she could wash dishes and mop. But he couldn't afford anyone; he had to do all the work himself. He finished, 'I tell you what—don't you go hungry. You come in here and eat and pay me later.' He added bitterly, 'Everybody else does.'

Judith was close to shedding tears of desperation when she went out to the street. What could she do? To whom could she turn? Then a brilliant idea struck her and she hurried to the bank.

'Mr. Bronson,' she said a bit breathlessly, 'I want to borrow some money. I am the owner of the homestead now, and I can use that for security.'

'I'm afraid I can't even do that for you, Miss King. I'm sorry, really I am. You see, mortgages are a drag on the market right now. I'm so loaded down with mortgages I just have to draw the line, refuse to lend a nickel on even the best of security.'

'But I wouldn't need much. Just enough to tide me over until the money that was stolen from me is recovered.'

'It isn't the amount of the loan; I'd just as soon lend you every penny the traffic would bear if I lent you a dime. It's the people I've turned down; people that I've known for years. I can't lend you money after refusing them. If I did, I'd lose every friend I ever made.'

'But would they have to know? Oh, I don't want to be underhanded about this, Mr. Bronson, but I do need the money so badly.'

'I understand, and I'm sorry I can't help you. Surely you have relatives in the East who will help you out temporarily?'

'Y-yes, I have; but I hate to go to them.'

She did not tell him that she lacked the stage fare to Sage City, where she had to go to wire; that she lacked even the money to send a telegram.

'If you really want work,' advised Bronson, 'the thing to do is go to Sage City. There's no stage until the end of the week, but you can get a man at the livery corral to drive you over.'

They just did not know. They just didn't understand that she was entirely without funds, without even a penny.

She thanked him automatically and went out. She did not know what to do. She had no money to spend for dinner and just enough to buy some soup for supper. She went dejectedly into the hotel. There she met Duke Fisher.

Duke said, 'Good morning, Miss King. Let's go over here and sit down; I want to talk to you.'

He led her near the big window looking out on the empty veranda. 'It's about that homestead of yours,' he said abruptly. 'Now that your money was stolen I suppose you'll give up the idea of a poultry farm. Or have you other funds available?'

She shook her head. 'I have no other funds, Mr. Fisher. As a matter of fact, I have been trying to get a job. But here in Juniper—'

'Then I'm sure you'll be interested in what I have to say. I'm thinking of going into the cattle business and intend to buy the properties on both sides of you. I'll need your homestead to complete my holdings, and I'm prepared to buy the place from you.'

'The homestead is not for sale, Mr. Fisher.'

'You haven't heard my offer, and you can't start poultry without money.'

'Mr. Hollister has promised he'd get the money back for me.'

'Mr. Hollister is a very optimistic young man. He's been hunting that bandit for six weeks and hasn't even come near to catching him. Even if he succeeds in getting him, your chances of getting that money back, I'm afraid, are mighty poor.'

'I don't want to sell the homestead,' she repeated firmly.

He ignored this. 'There are a hundred and sixty acres of land, a house, and a few outbuildings. I'll pay you a dollar an acre and five hundred for the buildings. That's a total of six hundred and sixty dollars. With that you could rent a place nearer Juniper with land enough for your purpose and stock it completely.'

She shook her head, her lips firm. 'I won't sell except as a very last resort. It isn't only the poultry farm; I was born on that homestead. I love it there. I want a job to tide me over. If I can't get one in Juniper, I'll go to Sage City.' She got up. 'Now if you'll excuse me?'

He rose with her and watched as she mounted the steps. He had not expected his offer to be refused. He could afford to offer her more, of course, but if she went to Sage City and got a job, she'd never sell, and when the railroad came through, she would profit, not he. He must keep her in Juniper where he could persuade her in some manner to sell.

He sat there and thought it through and reached a plan of action at last. It might work, but he would let her stew the rest of the day.

He saddled up and rode toward the Bitterroot. Henry Gardner owned the ranch north of the homestead and Henry would sell. He reached the place around noon and had dinner with Henry. Duke easily made a deal with him, buying the entire strip along the Bitterroot and paying him an option of one hundred dollars. Then he completed a similar deal with Abe Dillingham, owner of the ranch south of the King homestead. All he needed now was Judith King's holding.

It was late afternoon when he returned to Juniper, and when he went into the lobby, Harry beckoned him over to the counter.

'The King gal,' he said, 'offered me a ring for ten dollars. She said her father gave it to her when she graduated. Looked pretty good, but I told her I'd have to ask you about it.'

Duke's eyes glinted. He went up the stairs and rapped on her door. She opened it and stepped back, and he took off his hat and entered. When she had seated herself, he took the other chair.

'Harry just told me about the ring.'

She kept her face turned from him. 'I just want a temporary loan on it. I'll redeem it, of course.'

'There is no need to part with it, Miss King. I've just purchased the places on either side of your homestead, and I really need your place. I'll double my first offer, give you two dollars an acre and a thousand dollars for the buildings. That's surely generous.'

'I told you that I don't want to sell. At least not until I know for sure that Mr. Hollister is unable to get my money back from that bandit. All I want is a job—any kind of a job.'

He regarded her steadily, but she did not shift her gaze. She had not yet been properly softened up. Hollister would never get her money back and eventually would have to admit his failure. By that time...

'All right,' he said quietly, 'I'll give you a job.'

'Oh, will you? I can sweep out the rooms, make beds, even cook!'

'It isn't that kind of job. Harry takes care of all that, and there isn't enough of it to pay his wages, but I have to have somebody on duty here. The job I'll give you won't pay much at first, but it will give you board and lodging, and you'll be free except for a couple of hours every night. Can you sing?'

'Sing? Why—why, yes, a little.' She laughed nervously. 'I'm no Patti, but I've sung in the church choir.'

'Your audience won't be exactly a church congregation,' he said drily. 'I want you to sing at the Happy Chance.'

The color faded from her face. 'A saloon!'

'A very nice one. The very best of everything. It has a small stage and a piano player. You come in at nine, do a number, and get right out. Come back at twelve for a second turn. You can use the rear entrance if you want to, and you can slip out as soon as you've done your number.'

'But a saloon!'

'Don't let that frighten you. I run a decent place, and you won't be bothered. And you said any kind of a job would do.'

'But I—' she began doubtfully.

'Take it or leave it, Miss King.' He got up, put on his hat. 'I'm making you the offer because your father was a friend of mine.'

She considered. She had never been inside a saloon, but she had the dislike for one which every well-bred woman of her day had. It brought up pictures of drunken, quarrelling miners, tobacco smoke, liquor fumes, honky-tonk girls.

'Well?' asked Duke shortly.

Her chin went up. 'I'll take it. When do I start?'

'Tonight. If you haven't had supper, come with me and we'll talk about it while we eat, then go down to the Happy Chance and rehearse with the Professor. He's my piano player. From now on, you'll get your meals at the restaurant and they'll be charged to me. You'll keep this room, of course.'

In the restaurant they discussed the songs she remembered, and he selected the ones he told her would go over best. When they had finished, she went with him to the Happy Chance and he showed her the back entrance, which opened on one side of the stage.

The stage rose only about a foot above the floor, and on it was a fairly good upright piano. The Professor was a thin, dried-up little man with an infinitely sad face and long, slender fingers that seemed restless unless on the stained ivory keys.

There were no customers in the place, and the chandeliers had not yet been lighted. They rehearsed several ballads and folk songs, and Judith regained her courage and her poise as she sang.

She returned to the hotel thinking that it wasn't so bad, after all.

CHAPTER TEN

Brad took up the search for Jake where he had left off. He would get the Blackbeard and Judith's six hundred dollars if he had to devote a year to the job.

What he did not know was that time was so important; he knew that the loss of the six hundred had hurt her badly, but he did not know that she was so desperately low in cash.

He was a man, and a man can always dig up a meal of some kind, even if he has to ride the grub line to get it. It did not occur to him that a girl fresh from the East could not readily do that.

He ranged back and forth through the barren hills, looking for some sign of Jake's passing, working methodically and patiently. The third day out he found his first indication that he was on the right trail. He came across the ashes of a campfire in a wooded hollow. Searching about the camp, he found where a horse had been staked out, and then something that definitely connected both camp and horse with Jake.

In a clump of brush near the fire lay a woman's small beaded bag.

The bag was open and it was empty. Jake had taken the six hundred-dollar bills it had contained.

He pressed the search more eagerly and for a while succeeded in following Jake's trail. On the days that followed it told him that Jake was gradually heading back toward his old stamping grounds near Duke's claim. By Saturday he decided that he could save time by going directly there himself and lying in wait for the bandit. He cut back to the stage road and turned first toward Juniper to renew his supplies.

He rode into Juniper close to midnight, having pushed on through the darkness, and rode at once to the restaurant, as hungry as a bear after hibernation. The restaurant man took his order reluctantly.

'I was just goin' to close up. If I didn't need the money, I'd tell you to take up another notch in your belt and wait until tomorrow. I sure hope you like your steak rare.'

He went into the kitchen and Brad waited patiently. When the man brought in his food and put it before him, he straddled a chair and watched him eat.

'Seen anything of John Rutherford?' asked Brad.

'Not since the stage was held up. Reckon the driver told him you'd gone after the bandit. Have any luck?'

'Some. Miss King is still in town?'

'You just bet she is. You know, I feel sorry for that girl. She's sure up against it. Been all over town lookin' for a job. Came to me, but I couldn't help her out. Tried at the store and the bank and just about everywhere but Tony's barbershop. But finally Duke Fisher gave her a job singin' at the Happy Chance. Twice a night, at nine and twelve. Don't reckon she'll get rich at it, but at least she eats and has a bed to sleep in.'

Brad put down his knife and fork and stared at the man. 'That's no place for a girl like her!'

'I know, but what could the poor kid do? Oh, everything's respectable; she goes in the back door, sings, and beats it right away. The boys say she's right good. Sorta shy and scared, but she'll get over that.'

Brad pushed back the plate, got up, put money on the table, and went out. A savage anger had kindled in him, directed against Duke Fisher. Duke, with his influence and wealth, could easily have found something decent for her to do, even if he had to create a job. To a girl like Judith, singing in a saloon must be repulsive and humiliating. The more Brad dwelt on it, the angrier he became.

He heard her voice when he was still outside the entrance to the Happy Chance. She finished just as he reached the doors, and there was a bedlam of whistles and yells and clapping hands. He pushed inside and strode toward the crowd at the rear of the room.

★ ★ ★

The first five nights were not nearly as bad as Judith King had expected them to be. She was nervous that Monday, but there were few in the saloon, and they were respectfully silent while she sang, and they seemed appreciative. The crowd was larger on Tuesday and kept growing as the week progressed. When she appeared, men at the bar or gambling tables came up to the stage to stare at her. It made her uncomfortable, but nothing objectionable occurred, and her

101

confidence grew.

To Duke Fisher, she was doing entirely too well. He had counted on her quitting the job and accepting his offer to buy the homestead; he had not anticipated the determination she was showing. Time was speeding by, and in another two weeks the surveyors should be in the basin. He had to get her land before that.

So on this Saturday he had a private conversation with several burly and rather disreputable miners who had done bits of dirty work for him in the past. It was not much he asked of them—just throw a scare into the girl. The Happy Chance, he told them, was no place for Sunday school hymns. Ought to have something snappy. Muss her up a little, scare the hell out of her. She must learn to turn out the kind of stuff the fellows wanted. Put on the act at the second show, he told them. That would give her Sunday to think things over.

He walked to the hotel with her after the nine o'clock turn, said he was dog-tired and was going to turn in. She could manage the second show without him.

Now, with the second show, she sensed trouble coming. The crowd seemed more vociferous, wilder. Three miners in particular, men she had not seen before, were drunk and loud-mouthed. They started heckling her when she began her first song, and Duke was not there to protect her. She kept on, but she was scared.

She started toward the side entrance to the stage which led to the back door after her second number, but a big miner, one of the drunken ones, stepped up on the stage and planted himself in the entrance.

'Not yet, you ain't goin',' he declared loudly. 'Not till you sing us somethin' snappy. Somethin' like *Suzanny*. How about it, fellers?'

A shout went up. 'Yeah! Sing *Suzanny* for us!'

'I don't know all the words,' she protested.

The big miner lurched toward her. 'That's all right, sweetheart; I'll sing 'em with you. Strike her up, Perfessor!'

Judith gave him a frightened glance, then tried to dodge past him, but his big arm went out and halted her. He closed the arm and drew her to him.

'Let me go!' said Judith furiously. 'Let go of me this instant!'

'Now that ain't no way to act. All we want is—'

She struck him on the cheek with all her strength. He dropped the arm and staggered back a pace.

'Why, you little hussy! I'll take some of the vinegar outa you!'

Men were shouting and laughing, enjoying the fun.

She looked desperately about her. Men

were crowded against the stage, and there was no door on the far side. She heard angry oaths, saw men thrust to one side like brush parting before the charge of a bear. And she saw Brad.

A man in the front row stumbled forward under the impact of Brad's body, turned and aimed a swing. It never landed. Brad's fist caught him squarely on the nose, and he tumbled onto the stage. Brad leaped over him, his hot gaze on the big miner; he reached the man just as he put his hands on Judith. Brad grasped him by the collar and gave a violent jerk, and the man was pulled away from her. Like a startled partridge, she ran for the doorway and through it.

The miner roared an oath and let go a swing that caught Brad on the cheekbone and staggered him momentarily. The miner rushed at him, swinging again. Brad managed to duck, then clinched with the big man, fighting for time while his brain cleared.

The miner was strong and huge; he raised Brad off his feet and tried to hurl him, but Brad had a grip on his collar and did not go down. He let go with his right hand and drove a short, hard right into the man's belly. He heard a grunt of pain and leaped in while the miner was still off-balance and hit him with a right hook that would have knocked an ordinary man off his feet. The big miner simply blinked and stepped back, raising his guard to protect his face.

He should have got inside the man's guard and kept pounding at his body, but Brad was too mad to reason. He bore in, warded off another swing with his left forearm, and drove his right fist against the miner's mouth, then Brad put everything he had into a belly punch. The man grunted in agony and bent over just in time to catch a shot on the point of the chin. Brad saw his eyes glaze and let him have another in the same place.

That one did it. The man fell like a California redwood. He hit the floor with a jar that shook the stage.

Brad wheeled as two other mean leaped toward him, fists balled, mayhem on their faces. He did not wait for them to come to him; he leaped forward and let one have it. The man went over backward into the crowd.

Brad wheeled to meet the other, took a clip on the cheek and crossed with a right. He followed up, angry and unreasoning, drew the man's guard down with a left to the pit of the stomach, then put a straight right squarely on the fellow's nose. The man staggered back and tangled with the Professor, who had been watching impassively from his piano stool. The two men and the stool went down together. Brad strode forward, yanked the man to his feet, and put another right where it would do the most good. The man went down on top of the Professor and stayed

105

there.

Brad turned to face the audience. He had lost his hat, and there was blood on his face. He croaked, 'Any more?' and nobody answered. He picked up his hat, slapped it on his head, and this time he did not have to push his way through the crowd. Several men slapped him on the shoulder as he passed them.

Outside he splashed water on his face at the horse trough. He was still smoldering. Duke had not been in the saloon, but nevertheless this whole degrading affair was his fault. Judith King must not enter that place again.

He got his horse and led him to the stable behind the jail, then went into the office, lighted the lamp, and sat down on the cot to think things over. Judith must not be permitted to return to the Happy Chance, and that meant she had to have another job. Where? Sage City would be the place, but that meant it would be years before she could realize her dream of a little poultry ranch on the Bitterroot. Perhaps that dream never would be realized; the six hundred dollars probably was already spent.

There was only one way in which he could help her.

He pulled out shirt and undershirt and unfastened his money belt. He took from it six hundred-dollar bills, fastened it again. He put the banknotes into the beaded bag and walked to the hotel. Harry was lounging in a chair.

'Has Miss King come in yet?'

Harry was staring at him. 'Yeah. Seemed all upset and kinda wild. Went right to her room.'

'What's the number?'

'Six. But you can't—'

'The hell I can't,' said Brad and strode to the stairway.

Light showed beneath her door. He rapped, said, 'Judith?'

He heard her quick step. 'Is it you, Brad?'

'Yes. I've got to see you.'

He heard the bolt slide, then the door opened. She stood there looking up into his face, and he knew she had been crying. 'Brad! Your face! That man—!'

'Is doing as well as can be expected. May I come in?'

'Yes. Oh, yes! Brad, I can never thank you enough. I was just—desperate.'

'Forget it. And cheer up. You're not going back there again. Look what I brought you.' He took the beaded bag from his pocket and handed it to her.

'My bag! Oh, Brad!' Her fingers trembled as she opened the catch. 'My money. It's there. Brad, oh, Brad!' She flung her arms about his neck, drew his face down, and kissed him on the cheek. She stepped back instantly, color in her cheeks, eyes sparkling.

'Now you can tell Duke Fisher to take his job and jump into the Bitterroot with it,' he said.

'I will! I will! Brad, you caught the bandit?'

'No, I didn't catch him. I stumbled on his camp; he dropped this in his hurry to get away. I'm going after him again, but first I'll see you settled on your homestead. You'll need help to get started.'

'Will you really? Oh, I'd appreciate that so much. I'll pay you, of course. And here—' She took out the six bills, peeled one off, held it to him. 'Take this as a reward. It doesn't begin to tell you how grateful I am.'

He pushed her hand gently aside. 'You can't pay a deputy sheriff for doing what he's hired to do. You keep it; you'll need every penny.'

'But—'

'Put it away. I won't take a cent for just doing my duty. Now I'll say good night. I'll see you in the morning.'

He went away feeling warm inside, recalling the light which had come into Judith's face at the restoration of the money. He'd get it back. He'd find Jake and get it back from him. With all the Blackbeard had stolen, he must have some money cached away.

CHAPTER ELEVEN

Duke Fisher slept late the next morning, entirely unaware of how his plan had kicked back on him. He had been awake when Judith had come running up the stairs and along the corridor to her room, and he could hear her muffled sobs as she entered her room and bolted the door behind her. He smiled tightly at the thought that the boys had certainly thrown a scare into her.

Give her time to think; let her realize how hopeless was her dream of starting a poultry ranch. She could not get another job in Juniper, and there was no stage to Sage City for another week. She had no money, and if she asked for her wages, he would remind her that he had promised actually nothing but her room and board. There was no other way out for her but to sell the homestead.

He went to sleep then, so he did not hear Brad when he came to see her a half hour later.

Duke got up around ten the next morning and went downstairs for breakfast. 'How were things last night at the Happy Chance?' Duke asked Harry.

'You missed the fun.'

'Oh? What happened?'

'Big Red McKeever and two of his

sidekicks got messin' around with the King gal, and Brad Hollister came in and pinned back their ears. Red has a busted jaw, and the other two got sundry bruises and contusions. And there's a note there on the table for you. It's from the King gal.'

Duke saw a folded sheet of paper beside his plate. He picked it up, opened it, and read that since Mr. Hollister had returned her stolen six hundred dollars, she was leaving for the Bitterroot at once; therefore she could not appear at the Happy Chance any more. Thanks for the job, but she really believed she was not suited to the work.

Duke folded the note slowly. 'So Hollister finally caught that fellow Jake, eh?'

'I wouldn't know. I watched while she wrote the note, and saw him, but I ain't seen anything that looks like a big, blackbearded gent named Jake.'

'Where is Miss King now?'

'On her way to the Bitterroot. She was up early, and her and Hollister went to the store and bought a lot of grub and stuff; then Hollister bought that double buckboard you had for sale down at the corral and a team of horses and some used harness, and they loaded up and left for the homestead. She was drivin' and he ridin'.'

Duke ate his breakfast, and when he had finished, he went into the lobby just as T. Jefferson Mason and his bodyguard came in from the street. He raised a hand and halted them.

'Leave us alone for a minute, Quant. I want to talk to Mason.'

Quant went out into the kitchen, and Duke asked: 'How long before those surveyors reach the basin?'

Mason frowned. 'I don't know how much they've done since I sent the wire. That was just a week ago. They should reach the basin in another two weeks, and it will be another week before it will be known for sure that the line will run along the Bitterroot. I'd say that you have two weeks to buy the land you want. After the crew once reaches the basin, folks will be inclined to hang on until they're certain where the line will run.'

Duke nodded. 'I've already taken options, but I'll pay in full before that time.'

'It's understood, isn't it, that when the surveyors come in, I will be free to leave Juniper? I have some investing to do myself, you know.'

'When they reach the basin, you're free to go.'

He called Quant from the kitchen and once more turned Mason over to him. Then he went to the stable, got his horse, and set out for the mine. He had made just one visit during the week, and had found things going smoothly.

He mulled over his plans as he rode. The

111

King homestead must be secured if he was to realize fully on the railroad. He had tried everything he knew, but one thing. And that was force.

★   ★   ★

Out on the King homestead, Brad and Judith were working hard to get the poultry farm started as soon as they could. With Brad to advise her, the girl had purchased enough supplies to last a month or more. And with his doing the bargaining, she had bought the used buckboard and a pair of horses.

They ate together at the restaurant in town, talking and planning, and Judith insisted on paying for the meal.

'I can afford it now,' she told him. 'Brad, that meal you bought me was a life-saver. I felt pretty low that day, almost as weak as the soup I had.'

'I sure didn't know it was so bad. Judy, if you'd only told me, I'd have been happy to stake you.'

She smiled. 'I'm trying to be as good a fighter as my dad was.'

'Well, it's all over. Like a bad dream. We'll get straightened out at the homestead, do some repairing and build chicken houses, and then we'll drive around the country buying chickens where we can. We might be a while at it, but it's a cinch you can't gather eggs until you have chickens.'

'I know, but it's my big gamble, and I'm going to put all my chips in the pot. If we get some good laying hens, the eggs will start coming right away, and I should have money to buy supplies when these run out.'

'Suppose,' he said gravely, 'this thing doesn't pan out the way you expect it to?'

'I'd have to sell out, I guess. Either to you or to Duke Fisher.'

'I can't picture Duke Fisher buying a chicken ranch.'

'He's already made me an offer. He told me he was buying the places on both sides of the homestead. He needs my land to complete his holdings.'

'How much did he offer you?'

'His first offer was a dollar an acre for the land and five hundred for the buildings; when I turned it down, he doubled the amount. Two dollars an acre and a thousand for the buildings.'

Brad whistled softly. 'Over thirteen hundred dollars! He must want it mighty bad. Why don't you take him up on it, Judy? You'll never get an offer like that again. It's twice what I could pay.'

'For one thing, it's my home. I was born there. For another, I'm sure I can make a go of a chicken farm. And when I add butter and cream—' She stopped there, her eyes dreamy.

He smiled. 'You'll make a go of it, all right.

113

Now let's go out there and make the dirt fly.'

Judith drove the team and Brad rode his horse. They reached the homestead before noon, and both went right to work. Brad pried the boards off the windows and smashed the padlocks on the doors, for they had no keys. He made some repairs to the kitchen stove, and Judy cooked noon dinner for them. As soon as they had finished eating, she set about cleaning house, and Brad tackled the repair work.

There was a stable with four stalls and still some hay in the loft. He cleaned the place and put the horses inside until he could mend the corral. He set about changing the bunkhouse over to a chicken house, putting in roosts and nests.

When Judith called him in for supper, he found that she had cleaned the kitchen and prepared a really delicious meal. They worked until dark, then sat on the little porch and talked plans and improvements until bedtime. They said good night, and he walked to the bunkhouse, which would serve as his quarters until the arrival of the chickens.

By the middle of the week, the place looked quite different. Corrals had been repaired, roofs fixed, broken glass replaced. Brad made several trips to Juniper for things they needed, once using the buckboard in order to fetch lumber. That trip, Judith went along with him and bought material for window curtains. They were both happy in their work and in each other's companionship.

Brad cut saplings and trimmed them for posts, planted them, and stretched chicken wire to make a yard for their feathered flock. He had opened the valves on the water pipes, and they had a constant supply of cold fresh water. He was putting the finishing touches on the chicken yard when he saw John Rutherford ride in. The sheriff looked down gravely from his horse.

'John, I'm sure glad to see you,' Brad said. 'It's been a coon's age.'

'Yes, I know. Rode into town to look you up, and the bar-keep in the Happy Chance told me where to find you. He said you got Miss King's money back for her. What did you do with Jake?'

Brad looked toward the house. Judith was not in sight.

'Get down off your horse.'

When Rutherford was settled on a block of wood, Brad squatted on his heels in front of him.

'So you had to shoot Jake resisting arrest. Well—'

'You're wrong,' Brad interrupted. 'The nearest I got to Jake after that holdup was about a twenty-four hours' journey.'

John lifted a gray eyebrow and shrugged.

115

'When Jake took Miss King's six hundred dollars, he left her dead broke,' Brad went on. 'Not even eating money, though she never said. I promised I'd fetch her money back, and I meant it. I went after Jake and came to his camp. Her purse was lying in the brush. Empty, of course.

'I had to come back to Juniper for grub. I was going to show her the bag so she'd know that at least I was on Jake's trail. I hit town just before midnight...' And he told of hearing that Judy was forced to sing in the Happy Chance, of his going there, and of his fight with Big Red and his two pals while Judy got away.

'I wasn't going to let Judith King go back to that place,' Brad continued, 'but she was broke, and there didn't seem any way I could help her without—well, without putting her under obligations to me, or making her feel ashamed. So—' He broke off, spreading his hands.

'So,' finished Rutherford, 'you put six hundred dollars of your own money into that purse and pretended you'd taken it from Jake.' He glared at Brad.

'Now for Pete's sake, don't let her know that. I told her Jake got away but left in such a hurry that he dropped her purse. If you talk to her, back me up. It's just like a loan, only she don't know she borrowed it. I'll get it back from Jake if I have to chase him clear to

116

South America and back. I'm going after him just as soon as I get Judith straightened out here. She aims to start a poultry farm, and she'll make good at it.'

The sheriff was grinning and he put a hand on Brad's shoulder. 'You sort of restore my faith in human nature,' he said. 'I'll back you up from hell to breakfast. Now take me over and introduce me to the lady; I haven't had the pleasure.'

They walked to the house, and Judith came out to meet them. Brad introduced Rutherford, and Judith insisted that he stay for dinner. After the meal, Brad went to the stable with Rutherford to get his horse. There he unpinned the deputy's badge and handed it to John.

'From now on it's a personal matter between Jake and me. I aim to collect six hundred dollars from him, but I won't be hampered by being a deputy.'

John nodded. 'I'll put in your time and collect your pay. Get your six hundred, and deliver what's left of Jake to me—if any. And good luck.'

The next day Brad loaded the buckboard with crates he had built and started out on his chicken hunt. He drove to the Gardner place, and since Gardner had sold to Duke Fisher, found Mrs. Gardner willing to sell her flock. He paid for them with money Judith had given him, left the crates, and said he would pick up the chickens on his way back.

He followed the Bitterroot to the crossing and turned westward toward Sage City.

He paid the few ranchers who would sell chickens, and said he'd pick them up on his way back.

He reached Sage that evening and finished buying in the town itself. He spent the night at the local hotel and the next morning bought grain and mash for the flock and started back, picking up the chickens as he went on. He drove into the homestead yard late that afternoon with eight coops of chickens and two sacks of feed. It was almost dark when he and Judith sat down to supper.

'I don't know what I'd have done without your help, Brad,' she said. 'Do you think Sheriff Rutherford likes your working for me?'

'Sure, but it doesn't matter. I turned in my deputy's badge.'

'You're giving up the hunt for Jake?'

'No. It's just that my quarrel with Jake is a personal one, and I don't need to be paid for hunting him. I'm going after him again just as soon as I finish here.'

'One more thing I wish you'd do. Buy two good milk cows for me.'

'How's the money holding out?'

'It isn't. It's not supposed to. "Everything in the pot," I said. When you buy two cows for me, and milk pails and a churn and the

118

other things, I'll be broke again. But I have plenty of supplies, and I expect to start right in selling butter and eggs.'

The next day he rode over to the Gardner place, found that Mrs. Gardner had a couple of milk cows, and bought them from her. The next day he and Judith drove to Juniper together, and Judith bought the things she would need, including two long chains for staking out the cows.

It was Saturday, and when they had returned to the ranch, Brad said, 'It's time I started after Jake. You're all set to go, and there's nothing more I can do for you except fetch out your father's saddle. You can ride after the cows in the evening and then ride on to Juniper.'

'I'm sorry to see you go, Brad,' she told him, 'and I can't begin to tell you what a help you've been.' She took a twenty-dollar bill from her apron pocket and offered it to him. 'Your pay.'

'That's too much. A dollar a day and board is top wages for a hired man.'

He finally accepted ten dollars, knowing that she was independent and did not want to feel obligated.

They had picked up Tom King's rifle and six gun, which Rutherford had left at Juniper for them, and Brad warned her to keep them handy at all times and to lock up securely at night. She stood at the door and watched him until he had ridden over a distant rise, then turned slowly back into the house.

It seemed suddenly lonely, and she knew that she would miss Brad. But she knew that the best cure for loneliness is activity, so she busied herself with the farm chores.

CHAPTER TWELVE

Brad rode into Juniper after dark and bought grub enough to last him for another trip into the hills, bedded down in the jail office, and left early on Sunday morning.

He rode to the place where he had lost Jake's trail and started working westward from there. The country was much like that he had previously encountered, rocky, barren, and wild, with the sparse vegetation stunted and seared by the sun. He rode a zigzag course, keeping to the low spots, scanning the ground for signs.

The sun was low when he rode out onto a rock flat. There was nothing in the immediate vicinity large enough to conceal a man and a horse, so he started directly across it. Then his eyes settled on what might have been a distant boulder but was not, for it moved, slowly and erratically.

He saw a man stagger upright and wave an arm feebly before slumping to his knees. Brad sent his horse racing forward. The man was sprawled on his stomach when he reached him.

He saw a tortured, whiskered face, a miner's slouch hat, and red flannel shirt. One leg was doubled up, the other stretched out behind him. As Brad swung from his horse the man croaked one word: 'Water!'

Brad knelt beside the miner, uncorked his canteen. 'Take it easy,' he said. 'Just a swallow at first.'

He let some of the liquid trickle into the opened mouth, fighting the hands that tried to clutch the canteen. He pulled the canteen away and hung it on the saddle. He went back and asked, 'Anything broken?'

The other motioned toward the extended leg. 'Sprained ankle.'

Brad carried the man to the horse. He put him into the saddle and started across the flat, leading the horse. The stranger sagged over the horn, clinging to it. After a while they came to the edge of the flat and descended into a dry ravine.

'How far to the nearest water?' asked Brad.

The man motioned down the ravine. Brad halted the horse and gave the man a sparing drink. They went on, and after an hour the ravine debouched on a plain dotted with bunch grass. Ahead of them appeared a cluster of trees. There Brad found a small spring with a little grass surrounding it. He lifted the man off the horse, gave him another and longer drink of water, then unstrapped his bedroll, spread a blanket, and placed the man on it. He lay quietly on his back, his eyes following Brad's movements. Brad gave him another drink, then refilled the canteen.

'Hungry?'

'Ain't et since yes'day mornin'.'

Brad gathered some brush, started a fire, sliced bacon, and opened a can of beans. He filled the small coffeepot at the spring and set it on to boil. When the food was ready, he took some over to the man, who was now sitting up. He ate like a starved wolf.

Brad examined the injured ankle. It was discolored and swollen. He got a shirt from the roll, soaked it in the spring, and wrapped it around the injured foot. He fetched the skillet from the fire, gave the man half of what remained, and ate the rest with a spoon.

The man finished, gave a thankful sigh, got out tobacco and papers. 'Reckon you'd like to know why I'm in such a fix,' he said.

'If you feel like telling me.'

The man spoke slowly between puffs on his cigarette. 'Had a hos, rifle, six gun, and grub. Was headin' west to a minin' claim I once worked. Yes'day mornin', it was. Feller stepped out from behind a rock and throwed down on me. Big feller knowed as Jake. Got me five, six miles east of where you found me.'

'Go ahead.'

'Said his hoss had broke a leg and he had to shoot him. Told me to get down and turn my back. Took my hand gun. Rifle was on the saddle. He got on and rode away, leavin' me without grub, water, or weapons.'

He took a long draw on the cigarette. 'I knowed somethin' about this country, knowed this was the nearest water and that I must reach it before sunup. I started walkin'. Went all right until night come, then I fell into a dry wash, landed feet first on some rocks, and turned my ankle. I started crawlin'. I knew I had to get to this spring or be fried on that rock flat.'

He took another draw, punched out the glowing stub on the ground. 'Reckon that's all. The ankle kept swellin' and hurt like sin, and the sun came up, and I seen I hadn't crawled more'n a mile durin' the night. I had to keep at it. I was about done when I seen you.'

He reached for the canteen, took a long drink, restored the stopper, and held it for a moment, looking at it.

'Seems like I can't get enough. Funny, ain't it? Some fellers say that water ain't no good except to wash in. Just try doin' without it for two days.'

'This Jake,' said Brad. 'I've been looking for him for over a month. He's wanted for murdering Tom King.'

The man flashed him a quick look. 'Tom King? Jake murdered him?'

'Yes. Did you know Tom?'

'Used to run across him when I was prospectin'. He worked mostly northeast of here, in the hills on the other side of the Briscoe road. So Jake murdered him! For his claim, likely. Say, if you catch up with this Jake feller, don't shoot him until I get a crack at him. Promise me that, Mister—'

'Hollister. Brad Hollister.'

'Joe Hartwell's mine.'

It was a moment before the name registered. 'Joe Hartwell? Thought you'd gone back East.'

The man grinned sheepishly. 'Started. Got homesick. Took out about a thousand in dust and headed east. Got into a poker game at Hartsville. They cleaned me out, so I headed back here to get me another stake.'

'The way I heard it, a man named Duke Fisher grubstaked you and you took out twenty thousand. You gave him his half and started home with ten thousand.'

Hartwell stared at him. 'Where'd you hear that?'

'From Duke Fisher himself. He's working the claim you were supposed to have taken the twenty thousand out of, and he's struck it rich. Said he urged you to keep on working, but you wanted to go back home.'

'Why, the lyin' son of a gun! He never

124

grubstaked me to a nickel. I talked with him a couple times in his saloon. But I never gave him half of twenty thousand because I never had that much in my life. Now why'd he want to tell a lie like that?'

'The only reason I can think of is that he stumbled on Tom King's claim that Tom hadn't yet filed on. Since Tom was murdered, Duke wanted it to appear that he had known of the claim a long time.'

Joe Hartwell nodded slowly. 'Maybe. But, hell! If Jake killed Tom, what was Duke scared of? Tom's claim belonged to the first feller to find it and file on it.'

'There's no real proof that Jake killed Tom, just circumstantial evidence.' He told of the first ambush on the Briscoe road and what had followed.

'It must have been Jake that killed him, all right,' Hartwell said. 'But Duke Fisher findin' that claim so soon! Don't that change things a bit?'

'It does. Duke could have killed Tom that night, but he has a good alibi.'

'Well, then, Jake's your man, sure enough.'

Brad helped the prospector over to the spring and had him sit down and soak the swollen ankle. While he was doing this, Brad cut a tree limb and fashioned a crude crutch. Then he tore the old shirt into strips and bound the ankle tightly.

'If you'll give me a lift a few miles west, to my claim,' Joe said the next morning, 'I'll give you some money and you can buy grub for me at Juniper. Jake searched me, but I had a couple double eagles in my boot that he missed. I'll pay you for your trouble, too.'

'No charge,' said Brad shortly. 'I'll help you there, but I can't go to Juniper right now; I've got to get after Jake. I'll divide my grub with you, and we'll both run out at about the same time. Then I'll go to Juniper and buy for both of us. Suit you?'

'Fair enough, I reckon it's more important to catch Jake than for either of us to eat.'

After breakfast they reached Joe's claim within an hour, and Brad got water and firewood for Joe and divided his supplies. He left before noon, confident that this time he would catch up with the elusive Jake.

*   *   *

On that same Sunday morning Duke Fisher rode back into Juniper. He had added to his force of mine workmen and, under a competent foreman, gold was being taken out in quantity. The mine promised to be a bonanza.

The loaded ore wagon, accompanied by armed guards, had started for the Sage City stamp mills, and Duke rode with it as far as Juniper. When he entered the hotel he saw T.

Jefferson Mason and his bodyguard, Quant, seated there. They both appeared bored with each other's company, and Mason's face brightened at the sight of Duke. He got up quickly and went to meet him.

'The surveyors should be close to the upper end of the basin by now,' he said in a low tone, 'and I want to buy some land before the news spreads. Let's drive out and try to locate them.'

Duke agreed at once. It would take the surveyors only a week to work along the Bitterroot River; then the land stampede would be on. Within that week he must somehow acquire the King homestead, for if Judith learned that the new town was to spring up opposite the spring, she would never sell to him at a price he wanted to pay.

'It's too late to start today,' Duke said. 'We'll leave at dawn tomorrow and pack our lunch.'

At five the next morning the three set out. Duke and Mason rode in the buggy, and Quant trotted behind them on his horse. They stopped briefly at noon to rest and water the horses and eat. Then, at Mason's suggestion, they turned off the road and headed for a gap in the hills to the northwest.

'The rails will come through that gap and go straight along the basin for five miles or so before curving toward the Bitterroot,' he explained. 'If the surveyors have covered as much ground as I think they have, we should meet them in or near the gap.'

They reached the gap in a couple of hours and halted near a man who was using a transit, waving signals to another man with a cross-staff. He got the location he wanted, straightened, and turned to them.

'Hello, Mr. Mason,' he said. 'Thought you'd be around to check on us before this.'

'Men like you, Kelly, don't need much checking. How is it coming?'

The man gave Duke a quick glance. 'Everything as planned,' he said cautiously.

'How soon will you reach the Bitterroot?'

Again the man glanced at Duke.

'Don't be afraid to talk,' said Mason. 'Mr. Fisher here knows what we're doing. Duke, meet Pat Kelly.'

They shook hands.

'We ought to start cutting toward the river in about a week,' Kelly said. He drew a notebook from his pocket, thumbed through it, examined it briefly. 'We can make pretty good time in the basin. Incidentally, we had to make a few deviations moving through the hills. Found several places where we could take short cuts. With your approval, of course.'

They examined the book together, and Duke saw several land sketches that they seemed to understand, although he did not.

'That's good, Kelly,' approved Mason. 'I

should have caught them myself, but I wasn't using instruments when I first went over the route. I'll make the changes on my plan. Anybody question you about the job?'

'A few. I told them it was a state job.'

'Good! Now tell Mr. Fisher what the job really is. Keep your voice down; we don't want the man with us to hear.'

'You're the boss, Mr. Mason.' The surveyor lowered his voice. 'We're doing this survey for the Atchison, Topeka and Santa Fe Railroad Company.'

'Thanks, Kelly.' Mason patted him on the back. 'You're doing fine work, and I'll mention it to the proper people. Shall we go, Mr. Fisher?'

It was long past the supper hour when they arrived at Juniper and headed for the Elite Cafe. After their meal Mason took Duke aside.

'You're satisfied, Mr. Fisher?'

'Yes.'

'Then I'll ask you to release me from—eh—custody. I really must get busy buying up some land farther along the right-of-way. If I can find another farsighted gentleman like yourself, perhaps I can raise a bit more to invest. Will you rent me a horse and buggy for a few days? I'd like to start by ten tomorrow.'

'You'll find a horse and buggy ready for you at the corral.'

They shook hands, and Duke went over to Quant. 'He's in the clear. You can let him go. Now come up to my room with me. I have another job for you, and I want to talk it over.'

CHAPTER THIRTEEN

There was a good crowd in the Happy Chance that night as Duke sat with Phil Bronson and Sheriff Rutherford at a table. Duke ordered a round of drinks and said:

'Gentlemen, I have a proposition which may interest one or both of you. I'm selling my property in Juniper, and I'm giving you two first chance.'

'Selling out?' said Rutherford. 'Happy Chance and all?'

'Happy Chance, hotel, livery corral, store building—everything.'

'Duke,' grinned Bronson, 'has become prosperous. He's going to retire and count the money his mine brings in.'

'Not at all. The mine can take care of itself. I have a good foreman, and I'm hiring your old bookkeeper, Phil, to keep the records. And I'm not retiring. I'm going into the cattle business along the Bitterroot. I've had a taste of outdoor life, and I like it. I've bought out Henry Gardner and Abe Dillingham, and I hope Miss King will sell me her homestead some day. However, I can get along without it. I'm sure she won't object to my cattle grazing on her quarter-section, since she isn't going to use it herself.

'You can see now why I want to unload in Juniper,' Duke went on. 'Too many irons in the fire. I'll make you a good price, and when good times come back, the buyer will make a fine profit. Phil, you're a banker, and have the cash to invest; John, you're a bachelor and don't go around blowing your money. I thought you might whack it up between you.'

'I wouldn't want the Happy Chance,' said Bronson. 'It takes too much personal supervision. The hotel, livery corral, the store and other buildings—well, I might be interested if the price is right.'

'I could use the Happy Chance,' said Rutherford thoughtfully. 'I'm getting along, and I'm pretty tired of riding all over the county and sleeping under trees. I'd like to quit this lawman business and spend the rest of my days behind a bar. Let's hear some prices, Duke.'

Duke started high and came down. He came down a lot. He figured he could afford to, for after the new town had sprung up on the Bitterroot, property in Juniper would be practically worthless. That these men, his friends, would lose cut no ice with him. Over the table they made a deal and went down to the bank to close it. When they parted an hour later, Phil Bronson owned the hotel, the livery corral, the store and other buildings and John Rutherford owned the Happy Chance. It was agreed that nothing would be said about the change in ownership until later.

Duke returned to the saloon around ten o'clock. There were four men at the faro table where Quant dealt. Duke winked at the dealer, and Quant knew the time had come to play the game that would send him away from the Happy Chance apparently a bitter enemy of Duke Fisher.

Duke strolled around the room, came to a halt just behind Quant. Quant was playing a variety of faro called stuss, in which the cards are dealt from the hand instead of a box. Bets were placed, and Quant drew a card. It looked clumsy, but in reality it was skillfully done, because Quant had to make it appear clumsy.

'Hey!' cried one of the players. 'You drew that card off the bottom!'

'That's a damned lie!' said Quant.

'It ain't no lie,' said another. 'I saw it myself!'

'You don't call me a crook, you lousy tramps!' cried Quant and went for his gun.

Duke's fingers clamped about his wrist as Quant drew the gun clear. He twisted sharply and Quant loosed his fingers, dropping the

132

gun. Duke wheeled him about, still grasping his wrist.

'I saw you pull that card, too,' Duke told him. 'You know I don't stand for that. Get out, Quant, and don't come back. You're fired!'

He released Quant's wrist and pushed him away, and Quant leaned against the table, rubbing his wrist. Duke stooped, picked up the gun, punched out the cartridges, and handed back the gun. Quant took it, cursed, and stamped outside.

This carefully rehearsed act was designed to mark the end of the friendly relations between Duke and Quant; whatever Quant did in the future would not be traced back to Fisher. Quant was to do plenty, and was to receive plenty for doing it. To complete the illusion, Quant visited the other saloons, drank heavily while cursing Duke Fisher.

The following morning Quant saddled his horse, tied on a bedroll, and took the road to Sage City. He rode as far as the Bitterroot crossing, then turned northward. When he neared the Gardner ranch, he descended the bank and rode along the river's edge so that he would not be seen by Gardner or any of his men. At the King homestead, he turned into a wash behind the buildings, and a short distance beyond them he halted and dismounted.

He climbed the bank of the wash, lay down

133

on his stomach, and prepared to watch. Duke had told him that Brad Hollister was on the place, and he had to spy out the land before carrying out his mission.

He saw Judith working about the place. She visited the stable, and he heard a horse whinny a welcome; she went into the hen house with an egg basket and came out again; and several times during the afternoon she changed the location of two milk cows that were staked out with lengths of chain.

Evening came, and she led the two cows into the stable to milk them. Quant had not seen Brad all day and was convinced that he was no longer with her. Presently he saw smoke coming from the chimney, and he knew that the girl was preparing supper. She fed the chickens, then went into the stable, apparently to feed the cows and horses. When she finally returned to the house, he descended into the wash, ate some cold food, then returned to his post.

The sun went down and Judith entered the chicken yard, looked about to be sure all the brood was in the hen house then closed the door and latched it. Then she led the animals from the stable, watered them at the trough, and brought them back—all of which was perfect for Quant's purpose.

At darkness, light came from one of the house windows. Quant picketed his horse on another patch of grass, rolled up in his blanket, and went to sleep. Hours later, his mental alarm clock awoke him and he checked the stars. After midnight. He saddled his horse, rolled his blankets, and strapped them behind the cantle. He led the horse behind one of the buildings and tied him there.

He walked quietly to the stable, listened for a moment, then entered. Faint moonlight permitted him to make out a ladder which led to the loft. He mounted it...

After a few moments he scurried down, shut the big doors, closing the hasp over the staple and thrusting a stick through it.

It was then that he heard the first crackle of flames from the loft.

Running silently to the woodpile, he gathered an armful of kindling and carried it to the chicken yard. He put the kindling against a wall, took a bottle of kerosene from his pocket, poured the liquid over the wood, and struck a match. The boards of the old bunkhouse were as dry as tinder and caught easily. He ran to his horse, mounted, and rode to where he could watch both front and rear doors of the house.

He waited. He could hear the flames in the loft roaring, and he could see them through cracks in the boards. The end of the chicken house was blazing fiercely. There were muffled cackles of alarm, frightened neighs and bellows from inside the stable.

Quant smiled. Looked like roast beef and fried chicken tomorrow...

* * *

Judith slept soundly. She was a healthy young woman, and all that week she had worked unceasingly. Her life in the East had developed in her no sixth sense of danger, which brings a frontiersman out of the deepest slumber at the first inkling of the unusual.

The frantic squeals of the horses awakened her, and she opened her sleep-drugged eyes. Through her window came a light that she thought at first must be from the sun. Muttering 'Just a little longer,' she rolled over and closed her eyes. Then she jerked them open and sat up in bed, wide awake.

Those screams of the horses and the bellowing of the cows were frantic calls for help; the cackling of the chickens, sounds of distress. She jumped out of bed, threw a gown about her, and ran to the door, yanking out the stout bar. From the threshold, she saw flames leaping high into the air from the stable; to her right, the chicken house was bathed in fire. It was as bright out there as noontime in June.

She cried, 'Oh, dear Lord!' and ran toward the stable.

She did not hear the crack of the rifle, but

she heard the bullet cut through the air close to her. She stopped. There was another shot, closer this time. It was fine shooting, but she was standing still, and the light was perfect.

She started again for the stable, thinking in her misery that if her stock perished, she might as well die also. But she could not get within twenty feet of the door. She drew in a lungful of scorching air, felt her hair singe. There came a great flare as the roof fell in, and she staggered away.

Desperately she tried to get in the chicken yard, but the heat held her back. The frightened cackling had ceased; no longer could she hear the screams of the horses or the frantic bellowing of the two cows. She staggered to the trough, splashed cold water over her face and arms, then sat down on the ground and buried her head in her hands.

She cried until she could cry no more. The flames burned fiercely, then reluctantly died. Except for a subdued crackling and an occasional sharp pop, there was silence. The odor of smoke was heavy in the air. When at last Judith King got to her feet, there was nothing left but two beds of smouldering embers and the bloated, roasted shapes of two horses, two cows, and a hundred chickens.

She went into the house and lay on the bed. She was no longer crying, but she felt numb and stupid. Her dream was gone, and now there was only one thing to do.

It was four o'clock in the morning. She got dressed. There was no horse to ride. It was five miles to the Gardner house and ten miles to Juniper. She set out for town. She walked steadily, bitterness driving her. The sky ahead of her brightened slowly; the sun peeped over the distant hills at her, then rose bright and clear. It was eight-thirty when she entered town, dusty and disheveled, her new shoes scuffed and worn.

People stared at her as she walked wearily along the street. She looked into the jail office, but it was deserted. Brad was not there. She went into the hotel and saw Harry in the kitchen preparing breakfast. She asked for his boss.

'He'll be down in a minute. Say, Miss King, you look like you could eat some breakfast. Sit down. What in the world happened?'

'I was burned out,' she said tightly. 'I walked.'

'From the Bitterroot? Why, that's all of ten miles. Go on, sit down. I'll fetch Duke.' He pushed a chair toward her and went upstairs.

Duke came down almost at once. He appeared very much concerned. 'Miss King! What's this Harry tells me?'

'I was burned out last night. Somebody set the stable and the chicken house on fire. There were two horses and two cows in the stable, and a hundred chickens in the chicken house. They're all gone.'

'That's bad. How did the fire start?'

'The fire was set, Mr. Fisher. Deliberately set.'

'You're sure of that? Who'd do a thing like that?'

'Yes, I'm sure, and I don't know who did it. If the fire started in one, it couldn't have spread to the other. They were too far apart, and there was no wind. And when I ran toward the stable, somebody shot at me. Twice.'

'Oh, come now, Miss King!'

'I know what I'm talking about. Whoever it was didn't want me to save the stock. I couldn't have anyway; it was so hot I couldn't get near enough to open the door.'

'She walked all the way from the Bitterroot,' Harry interjected. 'I told her to have breakfast.'

'Of course. Harry, pour some coffee right away.'

Judith did not feel like eating, but she sat down at the table with Duke and went through the motions.

'Now,' said Duke, 'how can I help you? But first, I want to apologize for what happened that night at the Happy Chance. I wasn't there to look out for you, but you can bet if I had been, things would have been different.'

'It's all right. Mr. Hollister settled things.

139

Mr. Fisher, I'm licked. They wiped me out, and I haven't the capital to start over. You once made me an offer for the homestead; is it still open?'

'Well, now,' hedged Duke, 'some of the buildings are gone. You can't expect me to pay you as much as I first offered, can you?'

'Very well. Mr. Hollister asked me to sell it to him before you did. I know I can sell to him without any bickering.'

'Now wait! I haven't withdrawn the offer. Naturally, I tried to do a little horse trading. It's almost second nature with me. But I'll not bicker; I'll pay you two dollars an acre and a thousand for the house.'

'It's a deal.'

They went to the bank, where Judith executed a deed and took in exchange thirteen hundred and twenty dollars in cash.

'I suppose you'll go back East, Miss King?' Phil Bronson said.

She shook her head. 'No, I'm going to stay right here. I'll find something to do. Perhaps I'll open a dress and millinery store if I can find a suitable place.'

'I have just the thing for you,' said the banker. 'A nice little store on the other side of Doc Kline's house. I'll rent it cheap, too.'

'We can talk about it later. I want to deposit a thousand dollars, then I'm going to the hotel and get a room. You know, I'm really quite tired.'

CHAPTER FOURTEEN

As soon as he had Joe Hartwell settled, Brad set out for the place where Joe had been held up. With the directions he had got from the man, it was not difficult to find. A short distance away he came across the dead horse, the one which had broken its legs and had been destroyed by Jake. The rigging had not been removed, Jake having been content with the saddle and bridle Joe's horse had been wearing. There was no rope; if Jake owned one, he had taken it along.

Brad took out the severed honda which he had carried in his pocket ever since he had taken it from the tree and looked at it reflectively. The cut was clean and at an angle of about forty-five degrees; if he could find the rope from which it had been severed, he'd have the murderer of Tom King.

He began the job of tracking Jake, following the few prints that showed on the flinty ground. This time he had some help, for Joe's horse had a broken rear shoe which identified the trail as that made by Jake.

He followed that trail for three days, slowly, mostly on foot, sometimes spending hours after he had lost it before finding it again. His grub was running out and he saw no game with which to replenish it. Joe

Hartwell, too, would soon be out of food. He decided to ride to Juniper the next day and buy more. He guessed that the town was not more than five miles away in a straight line, and he could make the round trip before noon.

On Wednesday evening he emerged from the rocky country and entered a section with grass and a few trees. And now Jake's trail became easier to follow; for Jake, apparently satisfied that he had covered his tracks, rode boldly where the softer ground plainly showed the prints. Brad camped that night in a grove of pines which he knew he could find again without difficulty, and the next day he headed across the hills for Juniper.

And then, quite unexpectedly, his long search ended.

He entered another grove of trees and pulled down to a walk, the dead pine needles on the ground muffling the sound of his horse's hoofs. He reached the end of the pines and looked into a clearing, on the far side of which stood a small cabin with a broken-backed roof. Behind the cabin rose a cliff forty feet high, and against this the cabin had been built. His gaze went at once to the open doorway and the horse tied just outside.

He pulled up sharply, and as he did so, a man came through the doorway and saw him. He stood there staring for a moment, and Brad saw he was big and blackbearded and wore miner's clothes. It was Jake, at last!

Instantly Brad sent his horse charging across the clearing, drawing his gun as he did so; but Jake jerked his horse's slipknot loose and backed through the doorway, drawing the horse after him. Brad fired one shot, but he was on the back of a galloping horse, and to have hit Jake would have been pure luck. Before he could fire a second time, Jake had pulled the horse into the cabin after him. The heavy door slammed.

Almost at once flame shot from the paneless window and a bullet passed close to Brad's head. He ducked and swerved the horse, but one of the bullets stung him on a shoulder before he could put the blank end wall of the cabin between him and the rifleman. There he pulled up and dismounted.

He felt quietly jubilant, but at once he sobered with the realization that Jake had by far the better part of the deal. Jake had the food he had taken from Joe Hartwell, and he had a canteen of water. Jake probably had Hartwell's rifle and hand gun in addition to his own. Jake was protected by thick log walls. Jake could sit there and eat while Brad squatted outside and starved.

Brad tied his horse to a tree at the foot of the cliff, got his rifle, and walked to where he could see the front of the cabin, but not out far enough to permit Jake to pot him. He

143

hunkered down to consider.

This end wall had no windows, and it was quite likely that there was none in the other end wall. The back of the cabin was against the cliff. In the front was a door and two windows. If Jake came out he would have to use the doorway, for most certainly he would not leave his horse behind. Jake was effectively pinned down as long as Brad kept that doorway in sight. The question was, how long could he do it without eating?

He got up and walked to the corner of the cabin, his rifle ready. He called, 'You might as well give up, Jake. I've got you trapped. Throw your guns through the window and come out with your hands in the air.'

'If you want me so bad,' Jake replied, 'come in and get me.'

'I don't have to. When you get hungry, you'll be glad to come out.'

'I got plenty of grub; I ain't worryin' none.'

'It won't last forever, Jake.'

'It'll last as long as yours. Longer, maybe.'

'Jake, I've been trailing you for a long time, and I'm not leaving without you. Save yourself time and trouble and surrender. You'll get a fair trial for killing Tom King.'

'You're crazy! I never killed Tom King.'

'O.K. Then there's nothing to be scared of. Come on out.'

There was no answer. After a few minutes Brad returned to the rear of the cabin.

Time dragged. For lunch, Brad tightened his belt a notch and waited it out. It did not help when he saw smoke coming from the rusty stovepipe at the end of the cabin. Jake was preparing his dinner.

Brad's gaze went to the cliff behind the cabin. Its top was some twenty feet above the broken roof. Brad studied it, then shook his head.

If it was at all possible, he must take Jake before dark. There would be no moon until late, and before that Jake would make a break. He'd silently open the door, mount his horse, and bolt out of there like a cannonball.

In the middle of the afternoon, Brad tried again. 'I'll have help, before long, Jake. Rutherford knows where I headed for. He'll be here with a posse by dark or before. You can't kill all of us.'

There was no answer.

The afternoon wore on. Brad had staked his horse on a patch of grass, and now he led him to a nearby spring and watered him. He hoped that Jake would see him and make his break. Once Brad got Jake in the open, he could run him down. But Jake refused to take the bait, and presently smoke came from the chimney again, and a gentle breeze wafted the smell of sizzling bacon to Brad. That did it. There is nothing more tantalizing to a hungry man.

He took his rope from the saddle and

moved along the cliff until he found a place where he could climb up. Carefully he made his way to its top. He moved along the edge of the cliff. When he was directly above the sagging sod roof, he lay on his stomach and looked down. The vulnerable part of the roof would be the middle of the ridgepole where it had been broken.

He lowered the rope until its dangling end was about level with the broken part, then moved away and tied the other end to a scrub pine. He went back to the cliff's edge and carefully scraped away the loose dirt and stones, then lay on his stomach, grasped the rope, and let himself slide over the edge. When his feet were level with the lowest section of the ridgepole, he twisted around to face the cliff, and doubled his legs. Putting both feet against the cliff, he took a deep breath, and pushed with all his strength.

He swung outward and upward in an arc, turning his body, and at the end of the swing he let go, trying to hit the broken ridgepole at its weakest part.

He went through the roof as though it had been made of paper. Instantly he was enveloped in a cloud of dust and dirt. He closed his eyes and held his breath against it. Then he opened his eyes, his gun in his hand.

Jake was seated at a board table near the stove. A rifle lay on the table near his right hand. Before him was a tin plate of food, and

146

he held a fork in his left hand, an opened claspknife in the right. His mouth was open and his eyes popping as he looked up, unbelieving, at Brad. He had probably thought a boulder had tumbled on the roof.

There was no time to aim; Brad just pulled the trigger. His bullet hit the tin plate and Jake went over backward.

Brad hit the floor and went to his hands and knees. Dirt from the broken roof filled the room with dust as thick as the smoke from a wood fire. Brad sprang up and hurled himself toward the fallen Jake, near the table. He saw the flash from Jake's gun, but Jake, struggling up, could see no better than he could, and the bullet missed.

Brad made another dive and his head struck Jake in the chest. Jake went over backward and Brad got his arms about him. Both had dropped their guns. Finally Brad got astride Jake and fastened his fingers about his throat. He raised Jake's head and smashed it down against the packed earth floor three times in succession. At the third bump, he felt Jake go limp.

Brad heard the horse at the other end of the cabin lunging around, trying to break loose. He got up, found his gun on the floor, and put it into his holster. He located Jake's weapon near the chair, and threw it and the rifle through a window. Standing against the front wall was another rifle, and beside it, the second Colt. He threw them out after the first two, then went over and quieted the horse. When he turned, Jake was trying to get up. He went over, took the man by the coat, and jerked him to his feet.

'Stand by the table,' he ordered, pushing Jake so that he staggered across the room, brought up against the table. Then Brad told him to empty his pockets and put the contents on the table.

Jake produced a dirty handkerchief, tobacco, papers, matches, some horseshoe nails, a worn wallet, a few coins. Brad picked up the wallet. It had the initials J. H. stamped in faded gold letters. He opened it and saw several small bills.

'Where's the six hundred you got at the stage holdup?'

'Spent it.'

Brad raised his gun. 'Take off your boots, or I'll do it myself!'

Jake sat down, pulled off his boots. Brad examined them, then tossed them aside. At Brad's orders, Jake stood up, took off his coat, pants, then his shirt. No underclothes, no money belt.

'Socks.'

'No. Ain't no need—'

Brad slammed him on the mouth with his fist, and Jake sat down on the chair, hard. He lifted a foot, pulled off the sock. He shook it. Nothing.

'The other one.'

Jake reluctantly bent over, carefully worked off the other sock, balled it, and tossed it after the first. Brad stepped forward, picked it up, shook it, holding it by the toe. From it dropped six hundred-dollar bills.

They were dirty and damp from sweat, but they looked mighty good to Brad. He put them into a pocket. Jake said nothing.

Coat and pants lay on the table. Brad picked up the trousers, felt the pockets, dropped them on the floor. He picked up the coat. The outside pockets had been emptied, but when he thrust his hand into the inside pocket, his fingers touched paper. He drew out a letter and looked at it.

It was addressed to Miss Judith King at a Boston address.

'I tell you, I didn't kill Tom King!' cried Jake desperately.

Brad paid no attention. The envelope had been opened, and he drew out the letter, read it, fixed his hot stare on Jake.

'This does it. Tom King had this on him when you murdered him!'

'So help me God, I didn't kill him!' cried Jake. 'I tried to that mornin', yes; but I didn't circle around Juniper and lay for him that night. I swear to God I didn't!'

Brad advanced on him, his fist balled. 'Then where did you get this letter?'

'I found it. On Tom's claim.'

'When?'

'Right after Duke Fisher took over. Up there in that lean-to where you caught me. Tom musta dropped it, or—' He stopped, his eyes widening with a sudden thought. 'Yeah! Duke could have lost it there. By God, it was *him* that killed Tom!'

'Duke has an alibi for all that night. If you found the letter, why didn't you turn it over to Sheriff Rutherford?'

'When he and you was huntin' me for Tom's murder? That there letter would have cooked my goose.'

'Then why did you keep it?'

Jake wet his lips, hesitated. But under Brad's piercing eyes, he gave in with a resigned gesture. 'I figured that Duke done it, 'specially when he showed up on Tom's claim right after Tom was killed. When I got the chance to sneak into Juniper I aimed to see if I could sell it to Duke.'

'You're only trying to save your own miserable hide.'

'I didn't kill Tom! I swear I didn't!'

'You'd swear to anything. No matter; you're overdue to hang, and I've a mind to do it right now. Where's your saddle rope?'

'Ain't got none. Never had.'

Brad looked around, saw no rope. He was inclined to believe Jake about this. Some nice, fat blackmail was right up his alley.

'You're sure that claim Duke's now

working was Tom's?' Brad said.

'Yeah! I watched Tom while he worked it. Took out a lot of gold. Oh, I aimed to kill Tom and file on it myself, but I didn't. Hell, you can't hang a man for what he aimed to do, but didn't.'

'Where did you go after I chased you off that morning?'

'I headed back for Briscoe. Wasn't no use tryin' to bushwhack Tom after he was wise to me. I didn't dream the damn fool would ride to Sage at night.'

'All right. Put on your clothes,' Brad said, thinlipped. 'I'll hog-tie you for the night. In the morning we'll ride to Juniper, and see how things turn out.'

After Jake was secured Brad cooked himself some supper. He was hungry.

CHAPTER FIFTEEN

Duke Fisher had the satisfying feeling of one who sits on the top of a hill and contemplates his surroundings with the knowledge that all is his. He had cash from the sale of his Juniper property; he had cash from the mine; he owned all the land surrounding the spot where the new railroad town would be built. There remained only a few loose ends to secure. Chiefly, there must be left no legal loophole through which his victims could crawl and point accusing fingers at him.

The day after buying the King homestead, he rode out to the two ranches he had purchased and paid both Gardner and Dillingham in full. Then he returned to Juniper and went to his room. For some time he sat at his desk, reviewing events to be sure he had overlooked nothing.

As for Tom King's murder, he felt perfectly safe. There had been no witnesses, and Harry, the hotel clerk-cook-chambermaid, would testify under oath that Duke had been in the hotel when Tom had been murdered. Joe Hartwell had told Duke he was going back East, and no one had seen Joe depart. Nobody could identify his claim as the one which Tom King had first discovered.

Duke's deals with Henry Gardner and Abe Dillingham were entirely legitimate, as were those with Phil Bronson and John Rutherford. The fact that he must have had advance knowledge of the coming of the Santa Fe railroad mattered not a bit; it was simply shrewd business, and if people thought that he had taken advantage of friends, then the hell with them! Duke was too powerful to be bothered.

Burning out the King girl's place found him again well covered. He had publicly broken with Quant, and Quant had

152

apparently ridden to Sage City the day before the fire. Nobody would connect Quant with the fire, simply because the man had no possible motive for setting it. He had not even known Judith King. Duke had not yet paid Quant for the job, but that could come later.

He had made but one slip that he could think of, and that was losing the letter from Tom King to his daughter. He had meant to burn it, but, somehow, matches were never at hand at the time. But if it were found, all the finder would learn was that King had made a rich strike. He might associate this big find with the one Duke so quickly discovered, but he could not show the letter without drawing suspicion of murder upon himself.

No, Duke concluded, he was entirely in the clear and had two fortunes in his grasp: one even now pouring in from the rich mine, and the other—soon to be realized—from his investments along the Bitterroot.

Outside the hotel he started for the restaurant, then halted as he saw two horsemen enter the street. The first one was a big black-whiskered man dressed in miner's garb; Duke recognized him at once as Jake. Behind him rode Brad Hollister.

Everybody knew of the search for Jake, and now people came from their houses to stare. Duke went out into the street and halted the horsemen. He was smiling as he walked up to Brad and extended his hand.

'I see you've finally caught your man, Hollister. Congratulations!'

Brad ignored the hand. 'Thanks.'

'What are you going to do with him?'

'Put him in the jail and get word to Rutherford.'

'You should have put him away when you had the chance, and saved the county the cost of a trial.'

'Maybe. Get along, Jake.'

They rode to the jail, where Brad ordered Jake off his horse, took him inside, and locked him in a cell.

'You must sit and meditate,' Brad told him. 'Or maybe you've been meditating on the way. Want to change your story?'

'There ain't nothin' to change. I know I'm a dead duck, but I didn't kill Tom King.'

Brad had brought Jake back over the hills and stopped at Joe Hartwell's place. At the sight of Jake, Joe had hobbled from his shack with mayhem in his eyes.

'Let me at that polecat!' he demanded. 'I'll peel off his hide and flay the daylights out of him with it!'

'The law will take care of him. This belongs to you.' He tossed the wallet to Joe, who opened it and counted the bills.

'Only reason it's all here is because the skunk didn't have time to spend it,' Joe growled.

'Most of your grub is here in the saddlebags. It will tide you over until I have time to fetch more, along with your horse and outfit.'

Now, after locking Jake in the cell, Brad put both horses into the stable, fed them, and walked to the restaurant. Groups of men eyed him as he passed, and most of them spoke a greeting. In the restaurant Duke, seated at a far table, motioned Brad to join him. Brad had no desire to sit with the man, but to quell any possible suspicions Duke might have, he went over and sat down. Before he could give his order, Judith King entered and walked quickly to their table.

'Brad, I saw you from the hotel window. You caught him!'

'Sit down, Miss King,' invited Duke, smiling expansively. 'Have supper with us. We'll make it a celebration, and the treat's on me. Brad deserves something for his good work.'

'Thank you, Mr. Fisher.' She sat down with them.

The restaurant man took their orders and went into the kitchen. They were alone.

'How are things on the poultry farm?' asked Brad.

Her smile vanished. 'There is no poultry farm, Brad. I was burned out Wednesday night.' And she told him about it.

'It's such a pity,' commented Duke sadly.

155

'I can't begin to think of anyone who'd do a thing like that.'

'You say you were shot at?' asked Brad sharply.

'Twice. But I don't think the man wanted to hit me; he just wanted to scare me away. I couldn't have done anything, anyway.'

'You'll have to rebuild,' said Brad, thinking of the recovered six hundred dollars. 'If you haven't the money, I'll lend it to you.'

She shook her head. 'I sold the place to Mr. Fisher.'

'Why!'

'I guess I was desperate. Desperate and discouraged. Mr. Fisher offered me a very good price, and I took it.'

'I really wanted the place,' Duke said suavely. 'Maybe you've heard that I've bought out Henry Gardner and Abe Dillingham. I intend to go into cattle, you know.'

'What are you going to do now, Judy?'

'I'm not sure, but I think I'll open a dress and millinery shop. Mr. Bronson owns a small store that he'll rent me.'

Brad shook his head. 'Your whole heart was in that poultry farm. It's a darned shame. You have no idea at all who did it? What about that fellow Big Red at the saloon when you were singing? And the other two. I wonder—'

'You may have something there, Hollister,'

156

said Duke. 'I guess Big Red is pretty sore at you. Maybe he thought that by striking at her he'd be striking at you.'

'I think I'll ride out and have a talk with Big Red.'

Judith was alarmed. 'Don't do it, Brad. Please! Even if he did it, he'll deny it, and punishing him won't bring the stock and buildings back.'

Brad did not answer, but his mind was made up. Big Red and his companions were the only ones he could think of who would be low enough to deal such a crushing blow to Judith.

During the meal Brad pretended to have forgotten his threat to call on Big Red. Judith and Fisher asked him about Jake's capture, and he told them, making it sound like an ordinary incident.

'You took a terrible risk,' Judith told him gravely. 'If you had broken a leg in the fall, Jake would have killed you.'

'And if I hadn't done it, Jake would still be thumbing his nose at us.'

Afterward, Brad walked with Judith to the hotel. There were many things he wanted to do, but settling with the one who had burned Judith's stock and buildings came first.

He told Judith about finding and helping Joe Hartwell, although he did not mention Joe by name.

'He's short of supplies, and I promised I'd

157

take some out to him. Also I borrowed his horse and rig to fetch Jake in, and I have to return them. It's not far, and if I hurry I can get out there before dark. I'll see you tomorrow, Judy.'

They parted, and he went down to the Happy Chance. Except for himself and the bartender, there were only two men in the place. They were playing casino at the poker table.

Brad ordered a drink he did not want, then asked: 'I haven't seen that fat bald-headed tenderfoot who's been hanging around the hotel. Wonder what became of him?'

'I been wonderin' myself. Nobody knows who he is or what he was doin' here except that he had some sort of business with Duke. I was going to ask Quant, the faro dealer, but Quant ain't here no more, either. You've seen him—skinny feller. But Duke caught him dealin' off the bottom and fired him.'

'Yeah? When was this?'

'Last—lemme see. Tuesday. Yeah, it was Tuesday night when they had their run-in. Quant pulled out Wednesday for Sage.'

But Brad wasn't interested in Quant. 'Big Red been in town since I socked him?'

'Nope. He's up on his claim nursin' a broken jaw. Man, you sure did belt him!'

'Where is this claim?'

The bartender told him, tracing a crude map on a bit of paper. Big Red's claim was within a mile of Joe Hartwell's cabin.

Brad bought a drink for the bartender and went out. He crossed to the store, bought some supplies for Joe, took Joe's horse in tow, and set off for the cabin. He reached it before dark, learned from Joe the exact location of Big Red's claim, and left immediately.

There was a small colony of miners who worked claims on Dutchman's Flat, and Big Red's claim, according to Joe, was the third from the near end. It was almost dark when Brad reached the flat, and lights showed in shacks, tents, and lean-tos. Before the designated shack he dismounted. He did not knock; he opened the leather-hinged door and stepped inside.

Big Red and his two buddies were playing cards by the light of a lantern on the table. They stared at him as he stood in the doorway, Big Red with a dirty cloth running under his broken jaw and tied at the top of his head, the other two with marks of their encounter with Brad still on their faces. Brad moved forward, stopped near the table.

'One or all three of you set fire to Miss King's buildings Wednesday night. There's no use denying it; I've got the goods on you.'

'Huh?' Big Red appeared to be startled. He looked quickly at the other two, and they in turn exchanged glances with each other.

'*Whose* buildin's?' mumbled Big Red.

159

'Miss King's. The girl who used to sing at the Happy Chance.'

Again they exchanged glances, shaking their heads.

'What buildin's you talkin' about?' asked one of the others. He appeared completely bewildered.

'You know what buildings. Tom King's homestead on the Bitterroot. His daughter lived there.'

'The hell you say!'

'Is that who she is!'

Big Red was staring at Brad. 'Mister, if you'll shuck that gun you're so anxious to use, I'll make you sorry for what you done to me.'

'I've got no time for that now. I say one or all of you burned out Miss King last Wednesday.'

'And I say you're crazy as hell!' answered one of them. 'We had a miners' meetin' right here on Wednesday night. Couple fellers had an argument over boundaries, and we all met and settled it. We didn't break up till after midnight.'

'That's right,' said the other man.

Big Red said, 'Now get the hell outta here. We sorta joshed the gal at the Happy Chance, because somebody figgered she oughta sing somethin' more racy, more lively-like. But we never burned her buildin's. You can take what you call proof and jump in the crick with it.'

'You men stay right here,' Brad said, 'while I do some checking.'

He backed from the room, closed the door, went quickly to a window, and looked through it. The three men had picked up their cards and resumed the game. They did not appear at all concerned.

Brad led his horse to the cabin next door, and this time he knocked.

The miner who let him in grinned a welcome. 'Brad Hollister, ain't it? Sure am glad to see you. Been wantin' to shake your hand ever since you gave Big Red his needin's that night in Juniper. I'm Ben Wesley. Set down.'

'No time, Ben. Just want to ask you one question. Did you boys hold a miners' meeting on Wednesday night?'

'Wednesday? Yeah. Couple fellows—'

'Yes, I know. Were Big Red and his two friends at that meeting?'

'Yes, they were. From beginnin' to end, after midnight. Why?'

'Just checking. I'll be seeing you, Ben.'

He left and headed for Juniper. If Big Red and his pals had been here at Dutchman's Flat until after midnight, they could not possibly have ridden to the Bitterroot by two in the morning. So his theory had been wrong.

He wondered if the somebody who had

egged Big Red on was Duke Fisher. Duke wanted the homestead, and Judith had refused to sell to him; had he taken this means to scare her out of the only job she could get, discouraging her to the point where she would be willing to sell?

Brad did not think much of this theory. Duke could not have wanted the homestead badly enough to take such an extreme and dangerous method to get it. As long as Judith did not fence her land, his cattle would have access to her range, and he certainly did not need her buildings. It just didn't make sense.

But an hour later it made plenty of sense.

He found Sheriff Rutherford's horse in the jail stable and a lantern burning in the office. Brad put his horse into another stall and walked to the Happy Chance. He sensed excitement the moment he entered. Rutherford left a little knot of men at the bar and came to meet him.

'Fellow just rode through on his way to Sage. Came down from Mescal and cut through the gap at the north end of the basin. He ran into a party of surveyors and that fat man that's been stopping at the hotel. The fellow asked what they were surveying, and Mason told him.

'Brad, the Atchison, Topeka and Santa Fe is running a branch line through this basin. It's going to run along the east bank of the Bitterroot.'

162

CHAPTER SIXTEEN

Comprehension was not slow in coming; a lot of things were cleared up by that one statement of Rutherford's.

'Let's go down to the jail,' Brad said. 'We've got some talking to do.'

They went out, and John Rutherford said, 'I see you finally caught up with Jake. That's mighty good work, boy. I'll take him to Sage tomorrow. Where did you find him?'

'There's a lot to it, John. For one thing, I'm not at all sure that Jake killed Tom King.'

'No? Who did, then?'

'We'll have to figure that out.'

After the sheriff unlocked the jail door and they'd gone inside, Brad started by telling how he'd met Joe Hartwell and followed with the story of Jake's capture.

'Jake had this letter on him. Read it.'

John read it. He looked up and said soberly, 'And you say you're not sure Jake killed Tom? What more proof do you want?'

'Jake swears he found the letter on Duke's claim, which, incidentally, is the one that Tom King originally discovered. Does that mean anything to you?'

'Only that Jake's a mighty big liar.'

'Maybe, maybe not. If Jake killed Tom and

took the letter off his body, why would he carry such a dangerous piece of evidence around with him? Why didn't he destroy it right after he read it?'

John stared at him, stroked his jaw thoughtfully. 'I see what you mean. Got an answer?'

'Jake gave me one, and it sounds pretty good. If he found that letter on Tom's claim, it could mean either that Tom himself lost it or that Duke Fisher lost it. If Duke lost it, where did he get it? Jake thinks Duke murdered Tom, and he told me he was planning to try to sell Duke the letter. He thought he could tell by Duke's reaction whether or not he was guilty, and if he was, Jake intended to bleed him for all it was worth.'

'Sounds like Jake, all right. But, hell, Brad! Duke didn't leave the hotel that night. He's got Harry to prove he didn't.'

'Harry works for Duke.'

'Yeah, but—Brad, I've questioned a lot of guilty men in my time, and I think Harry was telling the truth. If he was lying, we'll never get him to admit it. And as long as we can't prove Duke wasn't there in his room, we haven't got a leg to stand on.' He got up. 'Maybe we'd better go down to the hotel and put Harry through the wringer.'

'Not yet. We've got to get more on Duke first. All we have is this letter Tom wrote that we found on Jake. Jake is the logical suspect, and we have a better chance of learning more if we don't tip Duke off.'

John sat down again. 'What's your idea?'

'A lot of things have happened that connect up, now that we know about the railroad coming in. You heard about Judith's being burned out?'

'Yes. I talked with her, and she said you figured it must have been Big Red.'

'I thought so, but I was wrong.' And he told John about his visit to Dutchman's Flat.

'That miners' meeting lets Big Red out. Now let's fit some pieces of the puzzle together. In the first place, Duke lied about that mining claim. Joe Hartwell denies that Duke ever grubstaked him; says the most Joe ever took out of his claim was about a thousand dollars. Joe also says that Tom King was working in the vicinity of the claim that Duke says he discovered about a week after Tom's murder.

'Now let's go a little farther: This fellow Mason must have tipped Duke off that the railroad was coming in along the Bitterroot. Duke goes out there and buys the land owned by Henry Gardner and Abe Dillingham. He tried to buy Judith's homestead, and she turned him down. Judith was broke and couldn't get a job in Juniper, and he knew it. He didn't want her to go somewhere else and look for work, so he gave her that job in the

165

Happy Chance. He hired Big Red to throw a scare into her, disgust her with the job to the point where she must quit. Not being able to get other work, she must sell the homestead to him. But my returning her six hundred dollars put a crimp in that. Incidentally, I got the six hundred back from Jake.

'She went out to the homestead, and I helped her get started. She spent just about all the money she had for stock and repairs. I left her on Saturday. On Tuesday night, Duke caught his faro dealer, Quant, cheating and fired him. Quant takes it lying down, which isn't natural in a man like Quant, unless he had agreed to do it beforehand.

'On Wednesday, Quant gets on his horse and leaves town for Sage City. On that same night, Judith's buildings are fired and somebody shoots at her to keep her from letting the stock out. You have one guess who did it.'

'Quant, of course.'

'Quant was supposed to be in Sage.'

'He wasn't!' Rutherford was becoming excited. 'I rode over here on Thursday. It was right early when I started, not quite light yet. Just outside of Sage I passed a rider coming from the direction of Juniper. I didn't recognize him until we were passing. It was Quant. He rode right by me without saying a word, but I guessed he hadn't recognized me. Brad, he's the man!'

'Right. But prove it.'

'We can put him through the wringer.'

'It wouldn't do any good. If Duke hired him to do it, he paid him enough to shut his mouth. Even if he says Duke hired him to do it, Duke will deny it. No, we've got to play it foxy, John. We've got to dig up some real evidence, and we'll never do it if we give Duke an inkling of what we're after. He's a slick article; he has big ears to listen with and a gold mine to buy things with. And now he has another gold mine on the Bitterroot.'

'You're right. But there's one thing that bothers me. If Duke knew a railroad was coming into the basin, why did he sell his Juniper property?'

'He sold his Juniper property?'

'All of it. Phil Bronson bought the hotel, livery corral, store building, and other buildings Duke owned. I bought the Happy Chance. Duke said to keep it quiet for the time being, but I don't mind telling you.'

'What reason did he give for selling?'

'That he was going into the cattle business and didn't want to be bothered with property in Juniper.'

Brad thought this over. 'John,' he said soberly, 'just what's going to happen to Juniper when this railroad comes in?'

'She'll boom. Bound to, with a railroad only ten miles away.'

'I'd agree if it wasn't for Duke selling out

and buying along the Bitterroot. John, suppose the railroad builds a station? It won't be at Juniper but somewhere along the right-of-way. If they do that, another town will grow up around that station. What will happen to Juniper then?'

John's face went blank. 'Good gosh, Brad! Do you mean that skunk unloaded because he knew Juniper property would be practically worthless?'

'I think that's just what he did.'

'Why, the low-down—!'

'He's all that and more; but if we're going to get anything on him, we've got to pretend we're the stupid fools he thinks we are. We haven't any proof to connect him with Tom King's death and Judith's burning out, but if he lost that letter he made one mistake. If we give him enough rope, he'll make another!'

'What do you think we ought to do?'

'You ride back to Sage with your prisoner. As long as you're around, Duke will watch his step. I'm a free agent now; I can stick around and keep my ears and eyes open.' He took the severed rope honda from his pocket. 'One thing I'll look for is a cut lass rope. Duke never carried a lariat, but if he shot Tom King, he must have used one to trip Tom's horse.'

'All right. I'll go back to Sage tomorrow and sit tight. I'll leave word where you can find me if you need me.'

In the morning, after Rutherford had left with his prisoner for Sage, Brad went to the hotel and inquired for Judith. Harry told him she had gone to look at the little store on the other side of Doc Kline's house, and Brad found her seated on an empty box inside the store. She jumped up and came to meet him.

'I'm trying to decide,' she told him.

Brad looked around. 'It's a nice little place, but I don't think your heart is in this hat and dress business, Judy. You have more money than you had to begin with; why don't you start another poultry farm?'

'I'm afraid. Somebody doesn't want me in that business.'

'Somebody wanted your place on the Bitterroot. Somebody who knew that the railroad was coming in. That's going to be a very valuable piece of property.'

'Do you think that Duke—? Brad, I can't believe it!'

'Keep on pretending you don't believe it. I'm going to find out who was behind that burning, but I never will if we tip off our suspects. I don't want Duke to guess that I'm trying to get something on him.'

They chatted a while longer; then he went out and walked to the bank. Phil Bronson came over to the counter and asked what he could do for him.

'Rutherford told me that you've bought property from Duke Fisher.'

169

The banker frowned. 'We were asked to keep that confidential.'

'Duke Fisher has forfeited your confidence, Phil.'

He told Bronson what he had told Rutherford about the new town. Phil was disturbed and angry.

'I never considered that angle, but you're right. Once a new town is built out there, Juniper will be dead. And Duke was supposed to be our friend!'

'He probably regards it as a smart business deal. Phil, what was the shape of Duke's finances before he found that mine?'

'That's something that I would have considered confidential, but now that Duke has swindled me, I'll tell you. Up to the time that miner he grubstaked made his lucky strike, Duke was broke. I held mortgages on all his Juniper property; he had paid nothing, not even the interest. I had given him notice of foreclosure, and he came across with that ten thousand just in time.'

'That ten thousand squared him?'

'Yes. A week or so later, he went into the hills and took up where that miner friend of his left off, and now he has bought land all along the Bitterroot where the railroad is coming through.'

'I see. Thanks, Phil. This won't go any farther.'

A web of strong circumstantial evidence

was being woven about Duke. If Tom King, believing Duke a friend, had confided the secret of his strike on the night he set out for Sage, Duke could have ridden ahead of him and ambushed him. Duke would have taken the location notice and the letter to Judith and subsequently would have 'discovered' the mine. But where had he got the ten thousand to pay off the mortgages?

Brad thought back to the morning after the murder. Duke's horse had not been in the hotel stable when he went out to feed his own, and Harry had said that Duke had ridden out of town on business. He must have ridden to the mine and got the money, making up the story about Joe Hartwell's strike because he dared not 'discover' the rich claim so shortly after Tom's death.

Somehow that alibi Harry had given for Duke for the night of the murder must be broken. Duke would have had to ride immediately after leaving Tom at the livery corral in order to get to the place of ambush before his victim. Could Duke leave the hotel without Harry seeing him?

Brad walked to the hotel stable and stood in its entrance, examining the hotel building. He saw the lean-to with its slanting roof just below the window which opened onto the hotel corridor. He saw a rainwater barrel standing at one corner of the lean-to, and knew that by standing on it a man could easily reach the roof eaves. This was the means of leaving and re-entering that Duke could have used. But still—where was the proof?

All Brad could actually prove was that Joe Hartwell had not given Duke ten thousand dollars. But Duke would counter that by frankly admitting he had lied because he had stumbled on Tom's claim so soon after his death and might make himself suspect. If only Duke owned a lariat with a severed honda!

Brad went into the stable and searched it thoroughly. He found several lengths of rope but none of the right size or recently cut at the right angle. Duke must have disposed of the rope, and in that case it could not be traced to him, even if it was found.

How about Quant? Did he own a rope and had Duke borrowed it? It was worth a ride to Sage to find out, and Brad started at once. He reached the Bitterroot shortly after noon and pulled off the road to a patch of grass where his horse could graze while he took a smoke and regretted not bringing anything to eat.

There was underbrush and some trees between him and the road, and the high bank of the river prevented his seeing the stream; but he heard the splashing of a horse as it crossed the ford and had a glimpse of the rider as he rode past an opening in the trees. That rider was the man he sought, the faro dealer named Quant. He was apparently on his way back to Juniper.

Brad saddled up and set out after the man, riding rapidly until he sighted Quant ahead of him, then pulling down to a pace that kept him too far in Quant's rear to be recognized. When they were about a mile from Juniper, Brad topped a rise to find that Quant had disappeared. The man must have pulled off the road.

Brad kept right on at the same pace, watching the hoofprints in the road before him. He saw them angle to the left and disappear into a growth of underbrush and stunted trees. He kept on and entered Juniper, sure that Quant would follow him.

Why was Quant returning to Juniper? Brad could find only one answer. If the quarrel between him and Duke had been faked, he was returning either for further orders or to be paid for those he had already carried out.

Brad tied his horse at the end of the street and went back into the alley, where, from the cover of an empty barn, he could watch the road and the range. He waited most of the afternoon but did not catch sight of Quant again. He knew the man had not entered Juniper, so he guessed that he was waiting for darkness.

If Quant had come to pay Duke a visit, it would be far easier and just as profitable to watch Duke. Brad first checked on Duke's horse, which he found in the hotel stable, then crossed the street and sat down on the store steps. Presently Duke came out of the hotel and went to the restaurant. Brad crossed the street and entered the restaurant himself. He waved a casual hand at Duke, who returned the salute.

Brad hurried through his meal and returned to the store steps. It was almost dark now. He saw Duke come out of the restaurant and enter the hotel, and Brad went at once to the stable and checked on the horse again to be sure that Duke had not gone out the back door. He decided to do his watching from here, for if Quant entered town, it was a good guess he would come by the alley. It was now completely dark, and Brad squatted down at the corner of the stable to wait.

An hour passed before he saw the dark shapes of a horse and rider stop at the lean-to, heard the man dismount. He saw a figure move to the rear door of the hotel, then an oblong of light appeared as the door was opened. Quant was silhouetted for several seconds while he stood listening, then he stepped inside and closed the door.

Brad crossed the alley to the horse, found a rope on the saddle, and ran his fingers along it until he found the honda. Unless a new honda had been made, this was not the rope which had tripped Tom King's horse. He put his hand into the saddlebags, and his fingers touched a bottle. He would have thought nothing of this, but a slight but unmistakable odor came from within. He withdrew his fingers and sniffed them. Kerosene!

He took out the bottle and thrust it into his pocket, mounted the rain barrel, and pulled himself up onto the lean-to and crouched beneath the window which opened onto the corridor. Quant had come up the stairs and was moving along the hallway. As Brad watched, he pushed open a door and went into a room.

Brad climbed through the window and tiptoed along the hall. The door of the room Quant had entered was closed, but he could hear muffled, angry voices. He drew his gun, turned the knob quietly, and stepped into the room.

'Hold it, both of you,' he said.

Duke was standing with his back to his desk; Quant was facing him, his back to Brad. Brad saw that back tense under the impulse to wheel, then relax again.

'What do you want?' snapped Duke.

'I want Quant for arson. He started the fire on Miss King's place.'

'That's a damned lie!' Quant spat. 'I was in Sage that night.'

'It's no lie. John Rutherford passed you on the morning after the fire. You were just entering Sage. It wasn't quite light yet, but he recognized you.'

175

'What of it? I was nowhere near the homestead.'

'The empty kerosene bottle says you were. I found it in your saddlebags.'

Duke said fiercely, 'You set that fire, Quant? I might have guessed it was somebody like you. First you cheat at cards, then—'

'Why, you dirty dog!' shouted Quant. 'You dirty, double-crossing skunk! Hollister, I'll give you the real dope on that deal!'

He turned quickly, his hands away from his body. Brad saw Duke's quick movement behind Quant, then heard the blast of a Colt.

The dealer's body jerked under the impact of the slug, and the anger written on his face turned suddenly to a look of disbelief, then agonizing realization. He stumbled forward one step, then collapsed, and as he fell, Duke put another bullet through his brain.

Duke looked at Brad over the smoking gun. He spoke calmly.

'He would have killed you, Brad. I think I saved your life.'

CHAPTER SEVENTEEN

There was nothing to be done for Quant; if Duke's first bullet had not killed him, the second one had. He had been killed to prevent his telling Brad about the fire. Brad

176

was sure of this, but choked back the angry words he was about to speak with the realization that the game must be played, as he had warned Rutherford, with the same guile Duke employed.

'I could have got him myself if it was necessary,' he said. 'It wasn't. His hands were empty when he turned.'

Duke threw open the cylinder of the gun he had taken from the desk drawer, punched out the empty cartridges, and replaced them with fresh ones.

'You didn't know Quant,' he said. 'He was chain lightning. It was an old trick of his, holding his hands away from his body when he turned. It throws the other fellow off guard.'

He put the gun back into the drawer.

'My ace in the hole,' he explained. 'It pays to keep that hold card hidden. You certainly had the goods on Quant with that kerosene bottle. I wonder why the damned fool kept it?'

'I'm wondering what he was going to tell me.'

'He wasn't going to tell you anything; he used that as an excuse to turn and let you have it. I could use a drink, and I guess you could, too. Come down to the Happy Chance and I'll buy.'

They went into the corridor and met Harry coming up the stairs.

177

'I heard a couple shots,' the clerk said. 'Went outside but didn't see anything. You two haven't been playin' with loaded guns, have you?'

'Quant tried to shoot Brad, and I had to kill him,' Duke said calmly. 'I'll send up a couple of boys to carry him over to Doc Kline's. Keep an eye on things.'

'You shot Quant!' gasped Harry. But Duke flashed a look at him and he added hastily: 'Yeah, I'll look after things.'

Brad and Duke walked to the Happy Chance. It was Saturday, and the place was fairly well filled, most of Duke's men having come in from the mine. Duke ordered drinks and explained to the men who stood near them.

'You boys know about the run-in I had with Quant. He came to town tonight and walked into my room. He was sore at me for firing him. Said if I didn't shell out a thousand dollars right away, he'd kill me. Brad here walked in on us and got the drop on him. He'd found a bottle in Quant's saddlebags that had held kerosene. Brad told Quant he was under arrest for burning Miss King's place, and Quant turned on him. I got a gun out of my desk drawer and shot him.' He raised his glass. 'Here's luck, Brad.'

Brad drank, thinking that Duke had had all the luck thus far. He had a pretty good idea that the thousand dollars Quant had demanded was payment for the job he had done, but now that he was no more, this would never be proved.

Duke said, 'Ed, take a man with you, wrap Quant in a blanket, and take him over to Doc Kline's. Have a drink before you go.'

Ed signaled a man; they had the drink, then left for the hotel. Brad offered to buy Duke another, was refused, so he went out and walked up to the hotel. Judith was sitting in the lobby, and he went over and sat down beside her. Her face was pale and drawn.

'I looked in the room,' she said. 'It was—awful.'

'I suppose you heard Duke's story?'

'I heard the men telling Harry. They're upstairs.' She gave him a quick look. 'They said Quant was the one who set the fire. Why did he do it?'

'Somebody wanted your homestead.'

'You think he was paid to do it? By—?'

'Yes to both questions. That thousand dollars Duke claims Quant demanded could have been pay for the job. Duke says he thought Quant was going to kill me; he wasn't—he was holding both hands a foot from his body. When I told about finding the kerosene bottle, Duke pretended to be indignant; he told Quant he might have guessed it was somebody like him. That made Quant mad, and he called Duke some names and said he'd give me the real lowdown on that fire. That's when he turned, and that's when Duke shot him.'

She nodded. 'Duke must have hired him, but you'll never be able to prove it now.'

'Maybe we can prove something else. I want to talk to Harry; when they come down, leave me alone with him.'

They heard footsteps upstairs, then the three men came down carrying the blanket-wrapped body. The two from the Happy Chance went out with their burden, and Judith went upstairs to her room. Harry came over and sat down beside Brad. He was sweating and mopped his face with a handkerchief.

'Quant a friend of yours?' asked Brad.

'Yes, and I don't give a damn who knows it.'

'When he turned on me, he wasn't going to shoot me. He had both hands well away from his body. Duke must have been pretty excited.'

'Duke's never excited.'

'Then why did he shoot Quant?'

'Why ask me?'

'Because Quant was your friend and you must have some ideas of your own.'

For a moment or two Harry sat with his lips compressed and his unseeing gaze on the distant wall; then he turned his head to look at Brad.

'I don't owe Duke a thing. I don't work for

him any more; I work for Phil Bronson. I'll tell you what I think, but you keep it to yourself. I think that feller Mason tipped Duke off that the railroad was comin' in, and Duke bought out Henry Gardner and Abe Dillingham. He wanted to buy the King place, too, but Miss King wouldn't sell. After she spent all her money stockin' up, Duke hired Quant to burn her out. I think he came back tonight to collect his pay and Duke shot him to save his thousand bucks. If you can pin that burnin' on Duke, you'll sure make me happy.'

'We can't prove that now, but there's something else we might get him for, with your help. The night Tom King was murdered you told us Duke came from the livery corral and went to his room and didn't leave it until the next morning. Are you sure of that?'

'Yes. I wish I could say different, but I can't. He said he wasn't feelin' good and was goin' to bed and didn't want to be disturbed by anybody. Came down in the mornin' and said he was feelin' fine. Right after breakfast he rode out in the country somewhere on business. Came back the next afternoon.' He flung Brad a quick glance. 'Were you thinkin' that he killed Tom? No, you wouldn't be; that feller Jake killed him.'

They heard footsteps on the veranda, then Duke Fisher walked into the lobby. He came over to them and spoke to Harry.

'Get water and a mop and clean up that mess in my room.'

Harry got up, went into the kitchen, came back with mop and pail, and mounted the stairs. Duke sat down in the chair he had vacated.

'Well, Brad, you got Tom King's murderer and the one who burned out Miss King. That about finishes things up for you, doesn't it?'

'All but a few loose ends. For one, why did Quant fire Miss King's buildings? He had no reason for hating her.'

'Maybe he made a play for her and she put him in his place.'

'She would have said something about it, wouldn't she?'

'No girl talks about those things except with her mother or another girl.'

'Then maybe somebody hired him to do it.'

'Who?'

Brad did not mind telling him what he thought, now that he could never prove it. 'The one who wanted her homestead; the one who will profit when the railroad comes in.'

'Am I to take that as a joke?' Duke asked stiffly.

'No. You knew she was broke and couldn't get a job, so you hired her to sing in the Happy Chance. Then you hired Big Red and his two buddies to disgust her and force her to sell. I put a crimp in that when I brought

182

back her six hundred dollars. You waited until she had spent that for stock and repairs, then hired Quant to burn her out.'

Duke stared at him, his eyes cold. 'The big hitch to that is that I publicly quarreled with Quant and fired him for cheating. He wouldn't have done a thing for me if I offered him ten thousand dollars to do it.'

'Unless that quarrel was faked. In that case you wouldn't have had to pay ten thousand dollars. One thousand would have been enough, don't you think?'

Duke's eyes were blazing now. 'You tell that story in the presence of witnesses, and I'll sue the pants off you, Hollister.'

'I just bet you would. But a lot of people think the way I do, and you can't sue them for thinking.'

Duke got to his feet, then stood looking down at Brad.

'I used to think you were a pretty good man, Hollister. A little stupid, perhaps, but still a good man. I've changed my mind. I don't give a damn what you or anybody else thinks. I don't have to. I'm working a rich mine, and when the railroad comes through, I'll be even richer. Phil Bronson hates my guts for unloading worthless property on him, and so does John Rutherford. Judith King hates me for getting the homestead, and you hate me on general principles. To hell with the whole bunch of you!'

183

He turned abruptly and strode from the lobby, and Brad heard his heels slap the boards of the veranda as he went out into the darkness.

Harry came downstairs with the mop and pail and went into the kitchen, and Brad thought briefly of going upstairs and searching Duke's room. He decided against this. When he made the search, it would be a thorough one, and he must wait until Duke was out at his mine.

Brad wished that Judy would come down, but she didn't, so he finally got up and walked to the Happy Chance. He saw Phil Bronson seated at the poker table with two miners and a stranger and went over to the table.

He said, 'Hello, Phil. Howdy, boys. Mind if I sit in?'

Phil said, 'Sure not. Sit down, Brad.'

Brad held up fingers to the bartender, drew out a chair, and sat down. The stranger was dealing. He was a strong-faced man of average size and build with keen eyes and deft hands. He wore a dark coat, dusty from riding, and a broad-brimmed hat, but his hands said he was not a cowman. They played a hand and Phil Bronson won. The bartender brought the drinks and with him came Duke Fisher.

Duke said, 'These are on the house. I'd like to sit in if I may.'

The two miners said, 'Sure.' Brad and Phil and the stranger said nothing.

Duke sat down between the stranger and a miner.

'How's the claim comin', Duke?' asked one of the miners.

'Good beyond all expectations,' said Duke. 'I'm going to put in stamp mills of my own and hire more men.'

'I see most of your boys are in town.'

'All but two guards.'

'Reckon you need them. From what your boys say, you've got a lot of dust and nuggets on hand.'

'I'm not worried. I bought a big safe and put it in my office for the dust and nuggets. It would take a freighter to carry it away. They wouldn't get far with it.' He tossed off his drink and picked up the deck.

'You're sitting pretty, all right,' said Phil bitterly. 'First a bonanza gold mine, now a big stretch of real estate along the new railroad. Not to mention all that you swindled John Rutherford and me out of.'

Duke was riffling the cards; now he stopped to look calmly at Bronson. 'I don't like that word "swindled," Phil. I offered my Juniper property at a fair price, and you and John bought without asking questions.'

'Why should we ask questions? You had advance information of the coming of the road from that T. Jefferson Mason. Instead of

185

sharing that knowledge with your friends, you used it to profit yourself at their expense.'

'Why should I share it?' asked Duke coldly. 'I don't mind telling you that I paid for that information. I paid a lot for it.'

'How much did you pay?' asked the stranger quietly.

Duke regarded him coldly. 'I don't see that that's any of your business, friend, but I don't mind telling you. I paid exactly ten thousand dollars for that information.'

'To a T. Jefferson Mason?'

'That was the man's name, yes.'

The stranger extended a hand across the table to Phil Bronson.

'Congratulations, sir. You weren't swindled; you got a bargain. My name is Preston and I'm with the Pinkerton Detective Agency. I'm looking for this T. Jefferson Mason. He's a swindler of the first water. You see, there is no railroad coming into this basin.'

CHAPTER EIGHTEEN

Phil Bronson broke the strained silence. He leaned over the table. 'Say that again, Mr. Preston. Say it slowly.'

Preston smiled grimly. 'Certainly. There is no railroad coming into this basin—no

186

Atchison, Topeka and Santa Fe or any other road.'

'That's a lie!' cried Duke, shaken out of his gambler's calm. 'I saw the plans myself; I even saw the surveyors running the line!'

'It's not a lie, sir. Anybody can draw up a set of plans, and surveyors can be hired by the hour or day. These were probably well paid by Mason to pretend they were doing the surveying for the railroad.'

'You say you're a Pinkerton man. Let me see your credentials.'

Preston drew out a case, showed him a card. 'I should think you'd be very suspicious of identifications, but this one happens to be genuine. Quite unlike the letter Mason showed you.'

Duke put his hands on the table and stared straight ahead.

Preston went on: 'I've been trying to catch up with T. Jefferson Mason ever since he pulled the same trick in Kansas. He was an employee of the Atchison, Topeka and Santa Fe but not a field engineer. He was a clerk in the main office until he was caught misappropriating company funds. He made restitution and was not prosecuted. But he was fired. He kept his pass over the line, but it has been voided. Also, he apparently made off with some of the company's stationery. The letter was written by him, and the signature at its bottom was forged. He pulled

187

this stunt in Kansas and got five thousand out of it. This time he doubled the stake.'

'How did you trace him here?' asked Phil.

'I was sure he'd try the same game again, so I studied the map. There were a dozen places where he might work, and I investigated them one by one. It took me several months to work down to this basin. Up near the gap I talked with a rancher who had seen some surveyors at work, but they quit some days ago. I rode into Juniper today and made some inquiries. I learned that my man had been here but had pulled out a week ago. He'll try it again, and the next time I'll nail him.'

Duke got up slowly. Like a sleepwalker, he made his way down the aisle between bar and gaming tables and went through the front entrance to the street.

One of the miners hurriedly left the table.

'I got to spread the news. Man, oh, man, will the boys enjoy this!'

'Me, too,' said the other, and got up. They headed for the bar, one of them calling: 'Hey, fellers! Gather round and listen to this!'

Preston said, 'Looks like we'll have to play three-handed.'

'Count me out,' said Brad. 'There's somebody I've got to tell, too.'

He left the saloon, passing the excited group that had gathered about the two miners to listen to the slick manner in which Duke Fisher had been swindled. They seemed to be enjoying it.

Brad walked quickly to the hotel. As he was crossing the open space beside it, he saw a man enter the stable. He passed close to the lantern which hung by the entrance and recognized Duke Fisher. He went into the lobby, looked around and saw nobody, and quickly mounted the stairs. There was a thin line of light beneath Judith's door, and he rapped softly.

'Who is it?'

He told her and she let him in. She was dressed and had been reading. He told her of the arrival of the Pinkerton man and his revelations about T. Jefferson Mason.

'Duke was taken by Mason for ten thousand, and paid you and Gardner and Dillingham more than the property is worth. He sold his Juniper property at a loss. Now he's a mighty sorry man.'

'He still has the mine.'

'He won't have that if I can prove—' He broke off, considering whether or not to tell her. He made his decision; the time had come.

'Prove what?'

'That he killed your father.'

She was genuinely shocked. 'But that man Jake killed him!'

He told her the whole story, then got up from the chair.

'I saw Duke going into the stable; he's

probably riding somewhere. I want to search his room, and I want you to be a witness to anything I might find. Are you game?'

'Yes, of course.'

'Fetch your key; it may open his door.'

They went along the hall to Duke's room. It was not necessary to use the key; they found the door unlocked. They went inside, and Brad lighted the lamp of Duke's desk. There would be no more fencing; either he found in this room what he needed to convict Duke, or he must concede defeat.

They made the search together, going through every item in the desk and bureau drawers, searching the closet, even examining the bedding and other places of concealment. They found nothing to convict Duke of the murder of Tom King.

'There must be something,' said Brad. 'I'm sure of it. Duke must have known where the mine was located; he got the ten thousand in gold he paid to Phil Bronson from it. Either Tom told him, or he got the location from papers he took from Tom's body when he took the letter.'

He was looking at the rope hanging by the window, the rope kept there for escape in case of fire. He was not conscious of looking at the rope, for his mind was on other things; but he was seeing it, and back in some recess of his brain was the image of a rope of a certain diameter, a rope that had been cut at an angle . . .

He snapped out of his reverie, his muscles tensing. The rope that Duke must have used to trip Tom's horse could be this one right here!

He strode across the room, put his hand on the coil, found the end. He turned.

'Lord! Judy, I've found it! Look!'

She came quickly to his side. 'What is it?'

He fumbled in his pocket with fingers that trembled; he took out the severed honda.

'The rope that tripped Tom's horse was a lariat. I found this honda tied around a tree. The killer couldn't loosen the knot and cut the rope. I've been looking for the rope, but Duke never carried a lariat, and that fooled me. See the angle of that cut? See how this honda fits it? Judy, *this is the rope!*'

They stood for some seconds looking at the two cuts. Then, in the tense silence, they heard footsteps in the hall. The doorknob turned, and Brad hastily thrust the honda into his pocket and drew his gun.

The door opened and Duke Fisher stepped into the room.

He was entirely composed, his old, imperturbable self again.

He had gone to the stable with some thought of riding far and fast but had changed his mind before he saddled the horse. There he had sat down on a feedbox to think things through.

He had been swindled by Mason, and both his pride and his pocketbook had been hurt. The hurt to his pride would never heal, but that to his pocketbook did not matter. He still had the mine, and it was a bonanza. Tomorrow he would ride out and stay there, superintending the digging of his gold. Nobody could swindle him out of that. To hell with Juniper and everybody in it!

He got up at last and went through the rear door to the hotel. Harry was in the lobby but paid him no attention as he mounted the stairs. He was deep in thought and did not notice the streak of light beneath his door. He was quite surprised to see two visitors standing by the window, one of them with a leveled gun.

He asked sharply: 'What are you doing in my room? Put that gun away, Hollister.'

'You're under arrest,' said Brad shortly. 'Close the door, then stand with your face to it.'

'Are you completely crazy? What is the charge against me?'

'Murder. Close that door and face it.'

Duke turned, closed the door, then stood facing it with his hands shoulders high. Brad walked over, ran a hand over his front, sides, and back but found no weapon. He stepped back, holstered his gun.

'You can turn around now.'

Duke turned. 'Let's get this fool thing

straightened out. Who am I accused of murdering? Quant?'

'Tom King.'

Duke laughed shortly. 'Now I know you're crazy. The fellow named Jake killed Tom. He even had the letter he took from Tom.'

'He found the letter on the claim where you lost it.'

Duke's lips curled. 'You're not only a fool, you're stupid as well. You can't even begin to connect that letter with me. And Harry will swear that I was in this room the whole night when Tom was killed.'

'All that Harry can swear to is that you didn't come down the stairs that night. You didn't. You got through the window at the end of the hall, slid down the lean-to roof and into the valley. You returned the same way, standing on a rain barrel to grab the eaves.'

'Nobody will believe a wild tale like that.'

'A jury will believe it when a few other bits of evidence are tacked to it. I'll give you a few facts to chew on. First, a witness will swear that the claim you were supposed to have discovered was really the one which Tom King was going to file on. Second, Joe Hartwell didn't go back East; he's here and he's waiting to testify that you never grubstaked him and that he never gave you a penny. Third, Phil Bronson will testify that you paid him ten thousand dollars two days after Tom's death, gold which you must have

193

taken from Tom's claim. Fourth, the man named Jake will swear that he found that letter to Judith on your claim. And finally—'

'Never mind the rest,' said Duke scornfully. 'Every bit of evidence you have is circumstantial and won't hold water. Suppose the claim I found had been originally discovered by Tom King. Tom never lived to file on it, so it belonged to whoever did. I guessed that it was Tom's, and that is why I lied about the ten thousand. I had no part in Tom's death, and I didn't want anybody to think I had. As to your witness Jake, who will believe him when he swears he found it on my claim? And even if they do, how can you prove that I lost it? Why would I be carrying a letter like that around with me? How can it be proved that Tom didn't lose it himself? Now quit this damn foolishness and get the hell out of my room.'

He had lowered his arms while he was talking.

Brad said, 'I didn't finish. There's one more piece of evidence that you can't explain away. It's so conclusive that when it's presented, the other evidence will be accepted by any jury in the West. Tom's horse was tripped by a rope stretched across the road. The one who used it couldn't untie the knot, so he cut the rope and left the honda part around the tree. I got that honda loose, and I've carried it around with me while I looked for the rest of the rope. I just found the rope it was cut from. There isn't any doubt; the angle of the cut is the same, and the rope fibers match exactly, strand for strand!' He stepped back, put a hand on the rope which hung by the window. 'This is the rope, Duke; the rope you used to trip Tom's horse just before you murdered him.'

For a few seconds Duke stared at him, searching swiftly for an answer and finding none. Flat denial was useless; the rope was right there in his room, had been all the time. To say that somebody else had used it was so weak as to be foolish.

Brad was talking again. 'You're a dead duck, Duke. That rope on the wall will hang you, even though another one is put around your neck. And with your conviction, the mine will go to Judith King. You can't keep anything you took from a man by murdering him.'

Despair gripped Duke. He had lost his property in Juniper, he had been swindled by Mason, and now the mine was lost to him, too. All he owned was some land along the Bitterroot, good only for grazing. He did not even have the cows to graze.

He could kill them; kill both of them, but that would not do. He must have time to get into the clear, lose himself so thoroughly that they would never find him. He made a quick little movement with his right arm, and a sleeve gun slipped into his hand; his fingers closed about the butt, and his wrist snapped the weapon up to cover Brad before Brad could snatch out his gun.

'I called you stupid a moment ago,' he said tightly. 'I was wrong. You're really clever, Hollister. I told you once I always carry an ace in the hole. That was on another deal, and the hole was the desk drawer; this time the ace came out of my sleeve. Now draw your gun, slowly, using only your thumb and forefinger, and drop it on the floor. If you make a mistake, it will be your last one. And then, of course, Miss King will have to go with you.'

Slowly, carefully, keeping his hard gaze on Duke's impassive face, Brad drew the gun and dropped it.

'Kick it under the bed. That's right... Now sit down in that chair.'

Brad seated himself. Duke strode forward, stopped four feet away from Brad, the ugly little gun pointed at Brad's head. He spoke to Judith.

'Take the rope from the nail, and do as I tell you.'

She flashed Brad a quick, apprehensive glance, then did as she was told. Under Duke's instructions, she tied Brad's wrists together behind the chair, looped it around a rung and tied it. Duke moved behind her and with the gun pressed against her back, told her the turns to make, the knots to tie in order to bind Brad securely to the chair. She worked silently, her lips tight, driven by her fear of the gun at her back.

When Brad was securely tied, Duke made her take the scarf from around Brad's neck and fashion a gag with it. Brad did not resist; no matter what happened, he did not want Judith hurt.

When the job was done, Duke made a careful inspection. He was satisfied. Then he went to the desk, opened the drawer, and took from it the gun he kept there. Then he crossed to the closet, got his six gun and belt, and put the belt around him.

'Now,' he said, 'Miss King and I are going for a ride. She will go willingly, holding my left arm. We will walk to the livery corral together. It's getting late and it's dark, so we're not likely to meet anyone on the street. At the corral she will wait with me while the hostler gets horses and saddles them. Then we will go for that ride.'

'No!' Judith exclaimed.

'Yes! If you resist or try to tip off the play, I'll put a bullet through you without the slightest compunction. Remember, Miss King, a man can only hang once; I haven't a thing to lose by killing you too. Behave yourself, and when we reach a place of safety, I'll release you. Shall we go?'

She gave Brad an appealing look, and he

nodded for her to do as she was told. She turned slowly and walked to the door. Duke opened it, and still holding the sleeve gun, he went out after her. He gave her the key, and told her to lock the door. He offered his left arm, and she took it, and they went down the stairs side by side. The gun in his hand disappeared.

'I can get it out in less than a second,' he whispered. 'Play it my way and there will be no trouble.'

They entered the dimly lighted lobby, and Duke crooked his arm so that her hand was tightly imprisoned. Harry was seated in a chair by the window but did not look at them. They went through the doorway, crossed the veranda, and went down the steps into the darkness.

It was very easy. At the hostler's shack Duke hailed, and the man came out carrying a lantern.

'Miss King and I are going for a little ride,' Duke told him. 'Saddle up the two best horses and fetch them out for us.'

The man nodded and slouched away.

'Don't make any mistakes or I'll kill you,' Duke warned the trembling girl. 'Get on your horse and stay right where you are until I mount. Be on my left side when we leave. Don't try to make a break for it; I can shoot you before your horse takes two steps; and believe me, I will.'

She believed him. He was a desperate man and had nothing to lose.

The hostler brought the horses and watched sleepily as Judith and Duke mounted.

Duke said, 'Good night, Toby. Don't wait up for us; I'll take care of the horses when we come back.'

The man said, 'Good night, boss,' and watched them ride away.

He yawned mightily, went into the shack, and stretched out on the cot. It was mighty nice of Duke, he thought sleepily, to be so considerate.

CHAPTER NINETEEN

Brad tested his bonds briefly and knew at once that he could not free himself. He rocked the chair, throwing himself alternately right and left until the chair finally fell with him. Once on the floor, he managed to roll to the door and with knees and forehead on the floor, made a series of thumps on the door.

It seemed hours before he heard footsteps coming along the hall. He heard Harry's voice say, 'What's goin' on in there?' but could only make animal-like sounds through the gag.

The footsteps went back along the corridor,

and Brad heard the thud of Harry's feet on the stairs. He came back at a trot, and Brad rolled away from the door as he heard the master key inserted in the lock. The door opened to reveal Harry holding a leveled shotgun.

Harry gasped, 'Holy smoke!' and leaned the shotgun against the wall and got to his knees beside Brad. He started fumbling with the knots, but they were too many and too tight to make fast headway, so he got up, mumbled, 'Got to get a knife,' and once more left the room.

He returned with a butcher knife and sawed at the rope until Brad got an arm free and was able to remove the gag.

He said, 'Duke Fisher killed Tom King. He's making a getaway with Judith as a hostage.' He was working at the remaining knots as he talked. 'Get a horse and ride to Sage and fetch Rutherford.'

He kicked free of the rope, gathered up the lengths, and thrust them at Harry. 'This is the rope he used to trip Tom's horse. Lock the pieces in the safe, and don't lose any time getting Rutherford.'

He fished his gun from beneath the bed and ran out.

At the livery corral he shook the sleeping hostler. The man sat up, blinking.

'Where's Duke Fisher?'

'He went for a ride with Miss King.'

'Which direction did they go?'

'South. Took the road runnin' south. Why?'

Brad left the shack without answering and hurried to the Happy Chance. He pushed through the doors, stepped to the bar, and hammered on it for attention.

'Duke Fisher is the man who killed Tom King. He's heading for the border with Miss King as a hostage. I want a posse, and I want it quick.'

He got it. Men ran for horses and guns, among them Phil Bronson and the Pinkerton man, Preston. Brad got his horse and led the way out of town, taking the road which led to the south. They rode hard, knowing they must close the distance between them and Duke before fanning out.

They had not gone far when Brad was seized with the conviction that they were following the wrong trail. Duke would know that with Judith to slow his progress he could not make a race of it. Also, if he intended going south, he would have taken some other direction first.

He halted the party abruptly, told them what he thought.

'He wouldn't take a chance going anywhere but straight south,' said Preston. 'He's wanted for murder, and he'll get to the border as quick as he can. If we catch up with him, he'll try to use Miss King to make a

201

deal.'

'With her in his hands, he can make a deal anywhere. I'm gambling that he's headed for the mine and the gold he has there.'

Preston said, 'If we ride to the mine and your hunch turns out to be wrong, he'll make it to the border hands down. I've trailed a good many men, and I say he'll keep straight south. It's his only chance.'

All of them but Phil Bronson agreed with Preston.

Phil said, 'I know Duke and I'll string along with Brad. I'll go with him to the mine; the rest of you keep south.'

They left at once, turning back to Juniper and turning into the Briscoe road. They rode hard and reached the trail leading to the mine just before dawn. They halted before turning into it, dismounted, and scanned the ground by the light of matches. There were fresh horse droppings at the foot of the trail, and the prints of two horses were superimposed on the older tracks.

'Your hunch was right,' said Phil grimly. 'Those droppings are not more than an hour old, and who else would use this trail at this hour of the morning?'

They followed the rough road as swiftly as they could, and after an hour they halted.

'If we ride together,' Brad said, 'Duke will know from the sounds that there are two of us. One of us had better drop a hundred yards or more behind. He'll hear just one horse then. I'll go first.'

'Let me, Brad. I'd rather have you as the reserve.'

'All right. As soon as you spot him, give him a hail that's loud enough for me to hear. I'll cut circle on foot and try to find a place where I can get him from the side.'

He waited until Phil was the proper distance ahead, then followed him. After another hour, Phil mounted the rise which paralleled the dry creek bed, then vanished on the far side. Brad was at the foot of the rise when he heard a shot and reined in abruptly. He heard Phil's raised voice.

'It's no use, Duke! I've got you pinned down. Better surrender Miss King and give up.'

Brad rode behind a cluster of rocks, dismounted, and anchored the rein with a stone. He took his rifle and cut at an angle for the creek bed, aiming at a point well above the mine buildings. When he reached the bank, he lay down and looked toward the claim.

The first thing he saw were two saddled horses standing outside the building where Duke had his office. One of them had a gunnysack lashed behind the saddle, and he guessed it held the loose gold from the safe.

The next thing he saw was a body lying in the middle of the creek bed. Another body lay in front of the bunkhouse doorway. Brad guessed that they were the bodies of the two mine guards. Neither Duke nor Judith was in sight.

Brad shifted his gaze and saw Phil Bronson. He was lying behind a rock on the top of the bank. His rifle was thrust over its edge, and he was watching one of the tunnels in the opposite bank.

If Brad was to get a clean shot at Duke, the man must be drawn out of the tunnel. That meant that he must form some sort of plan with Phil. He got to his feet and cut back to the trail. Silently he moved up beside Phil, covering the last few yards on his stomach. He put his lips close to Phil's ear and whispered.

'He thinks you're alone. Let him keep on thinking it. Where are they?'

Phil whispered, 'In that tunnel, or the lateral behind it. Too dark to see in there.'

Duke's voice came from within the tunnel: 'You out there! I'm coming out, and I'll have Miss King in front of me and my gun at her back. When you see her at the mouth of the drift, stand up, throw away your guns, get your horse, and come down into the wash.'

'Stall him!' whispered Brad. 'Tell him more men are coming.'

Phil called, 'You can't get away with it, Duke. There's a posse coming up the road right now.'

'You're lying. You're alone. Do as I order, or it's the end of the trail for the girl.'

'Do what he tells you,' whispered Brad.

He did not dare raise his head to look over the bank, for Duke would surely see him. He knew when they appeared at the mouth of the tunnel, because Phil called, 'All right; you win, Duke,' and got to his feet. He threw away his rifle and six gun. He turned and walked down the slope, got his horse, and led it past Brad and down into the creek bed. Sure that Duke's attention would be centered on Phil, Brad took off his hat and looked over the bank.

He saw Judith standing just outside the entrance to the tunnel with Duke behind her. He did not have to see it to know that Duke held a cocked gun against her back. He could see Duke's head behind that of the girl, the face haggard and strained with intensity, the eyes bright and glinting and fixed on the descending Phil. Brad knew that if he brought the rifle into firing position, Duke would surely see the movement and squeeze the trigger. Or would he? Brad did not know and dared not take the chance.

He released his grip on the rifle and drew his Colt. If Duke intended to shoot Phil as he had shot the guards, he would have to take the gun from Judith's back to do so. In those few seconds Brad would have his chance.

Phil led the horse to within six feet of

where Duke and Judith stood. He halted.

'My friend the banker,' Duke sneered. 'I'd like to kill you, Phil, but if there should happen to be a posse coming this way, they'd hear the shot. Take that horse over there with the others.'

Phil turned to the left with the horse, and Judith and Duke walked with him. Brad raised to an elbow but had no chance to shoot; the head of Phil's horse was in the way and Duke still held the cocked gun at Judith's back.

They passed out of Brad's view, and, difficult as it was, he knew he must wait. He thought swiftly. Duke and Judith would ride up the bank and past the rock which hid him. Judith would come first, and he must get Duke when she started down the incline on this side and Duke was just topping the rise.

He heard Duke say, 'Get inside. You will break out in time, but by then I'll be far away and you won't have a horse. Hurry it up.'

Brad heard a door slam, heard the metallic clatter of a hasp and staple. Then Duke said, 'Mount up,' and leather creaked as Judith got into the saddle. Brad heard the horses start, and he got to his knees, crowding the rock to remain hidden.

The horses did not come up the embankment! Later he realized that Duke would not take the trail and risk meeting a posse. He heard the rasp of hoofs on the dry creek bed, ventured a look just as they were passing. Duke rode on the far side of Judith, slightly behind her and with the gun only a foot or so from her back. It would take only a slight pressure on the trigger to send a bullet into her body, and that pressure would surely come at the impact of Brad's bullet. Or would it? Again he did not know, and again he dared not take the chance.

Duke was holding the rein of Phil's horse in his left hand together with his own; his right hand held the cocked gun. He was leading Phil's horse away so that Phil could not pursue him when he broke out of the building. Before Brad could think of a way to counter this unexpected move, they had passed out of his sight.

He swore in frustration, slithered back from the edge of the bank, and started running. He dodged around boulders, looking for a place farther on from which he could look down on them. There was a curve in the creek bed which permitted him to take a short cut, and beyond that curve he flung himself on the ground at the top of the bank. He heard the tramp of approaching hoofs and took a quick look. Duke was still riding beside Judith with the gun at her back, but he had turned in the saddle and was looking back toward the curve. Brad caught the movement of Duke's head and ducked back out of sight. The hoofbeats were right below him.

Brad was thinking desperately. This would probably be his last chance, but he did not dare risk a shot at Duke while he held the gun so close to Judith. How could the threat of that gun be removed?

Inspiration came. The led horse! If anything happened to it, Duke's attention would be distracted. If the horse were to stumble—or shy!

He let go of the six gun, and his fingers closed around a stone the size of a walnut. He raised his body and drew back his arm. The creek bank fell away at an angle of forty-five degrees, and the led horse was directly before and below him. And Duke had turned his head to scan the top of the bank to his left!

Brad threw the stone. It struck the led horse on the flank, and the animal made a startled jump to the side, jerking tight the rein which Duke held, pulling him off balance. He cursed the horse and turned to see what had startled it. And the gun swung around with him!

Brad leaped. He forgot the gun lying on the ground beside him; he forgot everything except that this was his chance to save Judith. Duke's horse had halted at the tightening of the rein and Judith was now a full length in advance of him. Brad struck Duke's horse like a boulder hurled by an avalanche; the horse went down, Duke went with it, and

Brad landed atop both.

Duke's leg was pinned beneath the horse, and his involuntary pressure on the trigger sent a bullet whining into space. He twisted his head, cried, '*You*,' and tried to arc the gun around.

He did not have a chance. The fierce fury in Brad and his pent-up fear for Judith released themselves in a mighty surge of strength. He seized the barrel of the Colt and tore it out of Duke's grasp; he raised it and brought the butt down on the black hat. Duke groaned, then lay flat.

The horse was struggling to its feet. Brad rolled off, got hold of the bit, and helped it up. And the next instant arms were around him and Judith's hysterical voice was calling his name, over and over . . .

*　　　*　　　*

Later that day on the hotel veranda, Judith and Brad sat as close together as two chairs would permit. Sheriff Rutherford sat more sedately in a rocker; Phil Bronson was sitting on the top step of the porch; and a goggle-eyed Harry was perched on the railing. Preston and his posse were presumably still riding southward.

'He must have gone quite mad there at the end,' said Judith as she concluded her story. 'He would have shot me, too. He had to save himself. When we were close to the mine, he tied my hands and feet and dragged me behind some rocks. Then he rode into the creek bed, and I heard a shot, and then another one just a few seconds later. The first came when he shot the guard who was on duty; the other guard was sleeping, and Duke shot him as the man was coming out to see what had happened.'

'He didn't have to shoot them,' said Rutherford. 'A man with his imagination could have cooked up some story to account for his taking the gold. After all, it was his gold to do with as he pleased. Like you said, he was plumb crazy; crazy with disappointment and hate and fear.'

'Well,' said Harry, 'he ain't so crazy as to escape hangin'. No jury would even leave the box. Everything's clear now, and it all seems so danged simple now that Brad put the pieces together for us. By the way, John, what becomes of the mine and the land Duke bought?'

'Judith is going to Sage with me and Brad tomorrow and file on it. The law says a man can't profit through murder; we got proof that the claim was found by Tom King, and there's no doubt that a court order will hand it over to Judith. Duke bought the homestead, but it won't be hard to get that sale revoked, seeing how it was manipulated. Judy, looks like you'll be a mighty rich young woman. What are you going to do with all that loot?'

'You'll have to ask Brad. He's going to be my—my business manager.'

'That's just another word for husband,' said Brad, grinning. 'We're going to be married at Sage. Me, I'm not a bit proud; I'll marry her in spite of her money!'